I0615584

Published by: Young Universe Productions

Text Design by: SHANON FLORETTA

Cover Design and Illustration by: FRANCESCO LEMOS

ISBN: 978-1-7340674-0-8

ISBN: 978-1-7340674-1-5

Distributed by:

Young Universe Productions
PO Box 1323
Midlothian, VA 23113

GLOW: AN ANTHOLOGY

WRITTEN BY NIKO SHEFFIELD

WITH ILLUSTRATIONS BY FRANCESCO LEMOS

YOUNG UNIVERSE PRODUCTIONS

To My Mama,

Thank you for it all. Everything has led me here. What a compass you are. Love ya.

In a similar version of your world, but a very, very different one, the Sahara Desert split itself open.

MAY 23, 1976, DON'T FORGET THAT DATE.

No one knew how or why it happened for a very long time. But one day it just opened right on up and released a pillar of hot energy that shot three miles into the sky for fourteen hours straight.

THEN, THE SHIT JUST VANISHED.

You can imagine that being weird to the world, right? Now that I'm looking back on it, I guess it really was kind of a spectacle. You know, I wasn't around when it happened...or was I? I'll figure all that out later. Well, anyway, it gets weirder.

Next, our Sahara desert did something we'd never seen before, it healed itself within two hours. It was like something out of a bible. It rained for forty days and forty nights. Grass started to grow, trees sprouted sixty feet in the air, a goddamn river bank formed, and now it's called The Sahara Forest. It's currently the main Eartian temple, so it's off limits to the general public.

Two weeks after the day that became known as "the Energy Split", there were reports of once-natural people from all over the world manifesting the ability to control the soil beneath their feet. But they could also control sand, concrete, bricks, mud, and a list of other natural compounds. See? Crazy right?

These people are now known as Earthers.

Then, three weeks from the day that became known as the Energy Split, there were reports of once-natural people having an ability to manipulate, generate, and emit solar energy from their flesh. Even crazier, right?

These people are now known as Lighters.

These were the new "sentient species" that just sort of sprouted up on our Earth among the many that had already walked it.

In a world full of naturals, and that's a common term used to refer to both Humans & Eartians, by the way, there actually was a time when life was super rough. Humans and Eartians aren't necessarily weak, they just can't tap into magic the same way that super-natural people can. Yeah, on our Earth, the super-natural plays a much more physical role than it does in yours. But once again, I'll get to that later.

Anyways, the universians found themselves feared by the masses. All the races in the world agreed to stop hating each other and banded together get rid of the "new threat." Both Lighters and Earthers had targets on their backs from the rest of the world. The most acute minds of the science-magic com-munity donned them as hypernaturals, a term the

Universians must've liked because they were very quick to civilize after that announcement. Whether they used to be Eartian or whether they used to be Human, each and every last one of them felt truly reborn as Universians.

The strongest among them came together and twenty-two Earthers pulled up two slabs of land the size of Egypt from under the oceans. One in the Ethiopian Ocean, and the other in the Pacific Ocean, dead smack on the planet's equator.

The country for the Earthers, the one located in the Pacific, that's Caldera. You won't always see it from space though because it's basically an underground network stretching up to every mountain. And as you could have figured, the land on the equator was for the Lighters. They named it Corona City and built a bridge to Ecuador since everyone there turned into Lighters. It's beautiful. Both places have been thriving independently without much assistance from outside governments. The Universians did manage to make a pact with the United Nations and the Wiccan Shadow Society. It stated there would be no broadcasting of any Universian politics through media of any format. Yep, that included social media too. The Universians lived in peace amongst each other for about twenty years. Only a handful decided to live amongst other mortal creatures in regular society, four million maybe. The other two and a half billion of them made homes on their shining, sinking and rising cities.

ANY AND ALL REPORTED SIGHTINGS OF THEM ARE IMMEDIATELY ERASED ONLINE.

But shit got really weird in 1994. There was a really strong rumor that the Universian races had broken their peace. Apparently the Earthers had declared war on the Lighters, so the story went. You can have your opinions on it after I lay out the full story, but to me, **THEIR WAR IS THE TURNING POINT FOR EVERYTHING.**

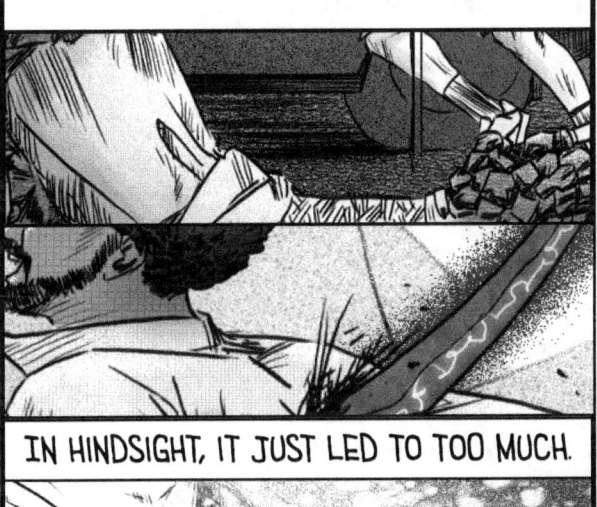

IN HINDSIGHT, IT JUST LED TO TOO MUCH.

CHAPTER ONE

THE MOON WAS RED THAT NIGHT

"Seriously," Rita said sternly. She pushed a long curly lock of jet black hair away from her face and smiled at him. He was being uptight again. "You gotta relax dude."

"Yeah, I know," Tevin said. He took a deep breath and started massaging his temples, groaning a bit while he did. He wasn't aware of the sound coming from his own body, and this caused Rita to start laughing at him. That smile of hers. Whenever he looked at her while she was smiling, it did something to him. There wasn't another single soul around them either. There they were, laid up on top of a blue yin-yang blanket to cushion them from the prickly bed of emerald green grass beneath them. Nothing around, only a bright red moon to eavesdrop.

They loved that field. I mean, it was the only one near their city to be filled with chocolate cosmos. All around them were drops of scarlet colored flowers that smelled like chocolate candy. The young love birds had managed to safely sneak out of the city and had made it to the lake. It really was a beautiful place, they definitely had a reason for it being their favorite spot in all of Corona. And it had just the right amount of edginess for them too, as it sat just outside of the city's district. In other words, they weren't legally allowed to be there. But the lovers were comfortable, and safely, alone.

"I just don't know why I'm here," Tevin continued. His eyes narrowing as he spoke, making his already thin face look even thinner. "What's the real point of my existence exactly? Do I have a choice in all of this? It's not fair that so much is riding on my shoulders yo. It's gotta be more to my life than just this here...shit almost feels pointless. I don't feel like my life is my own."

Rita stared at him for a little. She was fully aware of all of the reasons he felt how he was feeling. She knew she played a part in it too. She'd been encouraging him to get stronger, pushing him on and being the ultimate cheerleader for him. "Hone that shit," she'd always tell him with a smile, always in reference to what was literally sealed within him. Fact was, he had the glow.

They were only seventeen years old. And even if she wanted to pace it, Tevin was getting stronger. The truth was that some days, she wasn't sure if Tevin was actually getting stronger, or the glow itself. More recently, Rita found herself not wanting the young man to scale too quickly. But what she thought would've been excitement, showed itself to be fear when she noticed the very slight, very dim, definitely blue glow that was emitting from Tevin's hands. From the star filled sky that blanketed them, a stream of red moonlight began to shine down on them as if to spotlight their love. Only, it didn't feel like that to her.

No, this felt surreal. Both Rita's and Tevin's eyes began to glow with fluorescent white light. Seriously, it looked like candle-flame shaped light bulbs had been surgically placed inside of their eye sockets. Neither one of them said a word when they looked at each other. They were too busy finding beauty in the other person's face during such a euphoric state. The lake was throwing them an otherworldly sense of peace since early childhood. But this night, this was something else.

As they stared into one another's eyes, Tevin's questions about his purpose began to play back over and over again in Rita's mind. She started to think back to the day that Tevin's mother, the beautiful and legendary Selena Torch, asked her to be her son's "unofficial guardian." During a Saturday sunset while Tevin's mother painted in the garden, Selena informed a then fifteen year old Rita that her best friend, Tevin, possessed an immense power called the glow. It was a power strong enough to bring the war with the Earthers to a screeching halt.

"Make sure you watch my baby's back," Selena told her. Nine years had passed since that day. Tevin's mother died in battle, along with Tevin's father, Stefañio. With each passing day, Tevin grew stronger. At the same time, she watched him grow more and more tired with the war against the Earthers. She wouldn't be surprised if he tried to run away from all of it.

But Rita knew the golden child of Lighters better than anyone else knew him. And she knew that all Tevin really wanted out of life was to grow weed in solitude on a farm somewhere in Canada. Unfortunately, he also carried the burden of compassion. He cared for his people. And the fact was, his people needed him. It was a lot to deal with for a seventeen year old.

The young lovers continued sitting there in silence, eyes glowing, admiring how clear the stars seemed to them in the beautiful night sky as well as one another. Rita started thinking back to all of the times he'd been there for her at her lowest moments. Tevin always made it his entire day's mission to keep her laughing.

"Hey loser," she said while playfully pushing him. "I think we should really be together."

He laughed, and said, "The hell is your weird ass rambling on about now?"

"You heard me," she said as she playfully pushed him again, this time pushing her weight onto him. Looking him square in the eyes she asked him, "Time and affection. Chocolates and roses. All that mushy shit. You and me, together. What'd ya say? You in?"

"Chill with all that mushy shit," he said jokingly with a few chuckles.

Soon they were both rolling around in the grass, tumbling over one another just as they had when they were younger. When they were finished with their playful bout, bodies all covered in dirt and grass, and the sweet smell of the scarlet colored chocolate-cosmos petals, the young man stood up. Tevin didn't know why, but he was compelled to stare at the full red moon. Two drops of rain hit his cheek, and he snapped out of his trance.

"Just like we're kids again, right?" she said with a giggle. He chuckled and suddenly fell back into his gaze upon the moon. As Tevin stared above him, his hands began to glow with a reddish orange light. Thing is, the energy emitted from a Lighter is always white.

Knowing what this meant, Rita rushed over to face him. Her eyes had stopped glowing after their roll around session, but Tevin's were still very illuminated. Much like his hands, his eyes were glowing a bright, reddish-orange tint. With the hopes of stopping him from reaching his full glow too soon, she tackled him and landed on his face, parting her lips slightly before she kissed him. She grabbed his hand, which was still warm, but was definitely cooling off. She loved him, so it was easy for her to do her duty and protect him. Tevin was the key to winning their war. She was proud to be his guardian, even if he didn't know that she was.

With a wide smile, Tevin looked Rita square into her deep brown eyes and said, "I'm in."

CHAPTER TWO

LYCANTHROPE
VIDEO NO.23

If you're watching this, that means that my discovery has already come to light in the world and I may be dead…but hopefully I'm not because that would suck. My name is Matt Scathers, and I discovered the first chupacabra. It was also the night that I found out that everything we'd been hearing about is totally real. There's a war going on right beside us, and I'm the one who has the proof. That's right, me. Well, me and my cousin.

On May 23, 2014 I got a phone call from my mother telling me that I needed to call my cousin Jackie to see how she was doing. Apparently, someone had broken into my Uncle Boogie's farm and slaughtered all of his goats. As much as I make fun of a mixed Black/

Filipino family being goat farmers, I couldn't find any humor in them losing out on their main source of income like that. Jackie's like a sister to me, and she's the only other cousin I have that's also half Nigerian and half Filipino. So even though I didn't want to go initially, I agreed to visit upon her request. So I packed up my shit to go stay with my aunt and uncle for a while to keep my homie company.

When I arrived at the train station, my aunt and uncle were waiting patiently for me. At 4:37p.m. I grabbed my duffle bag, stepped onto the soil of Darling's Towne, South Carolina, and waved hello to my second family. They rushed me, taking my bag from me and embracing me in beautiful over dramatic fashion.

"Hey there, Matt," my Uncle Boogie said with his tight eyes and huge ass smile. He embraced me in a bearhug. "My sister's doing okay with feeding you I see. Seems like you get taller every year."

"C'mon now, you know its just a little puberty," I said laughing. "Hey Uncle Boogie. Hey Auntie Angela, how's everything?"

I welcomed a tight knit hug from my aunt, whose rich brown skin smelled of coca butter and lavender. A piece of her coiled black hair got stuck in my right earring.

"I'm...not going to lie to you, I'm scared shitless," She replied bluntly as she pulled her hair off of my head. I chuckled at the look of my uncle's facial expression during all of this and my aunt started laughing a bit too. She didn't cuss much in public, or anywhere for the most part, so it kind of threw us both off. Awkward as it were, we were trying to make the best of a particularly strange moment. Even if all of us were scared shitless.

My family is typically comprised of good-natured country folk and smart-aleck city goers. I'm part of the latter. I don't know my Filipino side that well, but the Scathers family is vast, hilarious, and tight-knit. I still find it crazy how my mom's brother fell in love with my dad's sister. But hey, life can be cool like that sometimes.

"Why are you guys still goat farming anyways?" I ask them, honestly not knowing why they did.

"Because it's profitable as hell," Uncle Boogie told me with another chuckle. "Hipster kids love goat milk. And goat cheese. All of that goaty goat shit, man. Fancy restaurants, cafés. The list goes on, Matty."

I couldnt help but laugh, I knew that shit was the truth. I love goat milk. My aunt Angela just shook her head a bit, trying not to laugh all flirtatiously at my uncle. Even with as long as they'd been together, the physical attraction between those two always felt brand new.

"Let's get you back home, shall we?" she said sweetly aloud.

On the way to their house I thought about the conversation I had with my mother at the train station. Before arriving to my aunt and uncle's, I had truly been trying my hardest not to go. I mean, the summer had just about started for real and I'm from Miami. You feel me already, right? Honestly, at that time, I didn't want to kick off my adventurous three months by catering to my spooked out cousin right before school let out. Didn't really seem like positive foreshadowing.

"Why do I have to go visit her?" I had asked my mother. "I hate South Carolina."

"Don't talk about your home-state that way, Matty," she said pointing her finger in my direction. "Your aunt and uncle say that

Jackie is really scared so you're going to spend a week with her so that she feels better."

"Why can't she come here? That makes more sense."

"They don't have the funds right now."

"Well then, you pay for it."

"Hell to the goddamn no, Matty," she told me with the ultimate level of ghetto feistiness her Filipino ancestors would allow her to summon. "I'm not gonna look after two wild ass sixteen-year-olds for a whole damn week during a summer in Dade County. Getcho ass on the motherfuckin' train. Love you."

With that last statement, she kissed me on the forehead and I hopped aboard. As unhappy as I was, I was still getting to see some close family members, and it was only for a week so it shouldn't be that bad, or at least, so I thought.

As we hopped into the shiny old 1995 grey Mustang that my uncle has had for what feels like forever, I realized how much I never really liked it here. Darling's Towne always had this weird energy to it that I could never quite put my finger on. The fact that something came out of the woodworks to slaughter a herd of goats didn't really shock me, but that's only because it was happening in fucking Darling's Towne, SC.

We pulled up to the large blue and white house that's pretty much been my second home since I began visiting when I was five. My cousin, Jackie, was on the front porch chillin' in a hammock. She didn't seem so freaked out at that moment.

"Jackie!" my uncle called out to my cousin. "Matty's here!"

When she heard that, my cousin poked her head up and looked in my direction with those chinky eyes of hers. She waved at me and laid her head back down on the hammock. Apparently I wasn't about to get the loud, over-the-top greeting that I usually get from her when I visit. I knew then that something was wrong.

"She's still a bit shook up," Aunt Angela said lowly. "She caught the tail end of it, when the animal was running off."

"I didn't know that part," I tell them. "I see why she's freaked out."

"We all are," Uncle Boogie said slapping my shoulder. "Come on in, we'll fix you a plate."

After placing my stuff in my room, I headed downstairs for a huge country style feast. As I grabbed my aunt's signature buttery biscuits and indulged in the lovely sweet potatoes, over-sized crab cakes, collard greens, and deep-fried turkey, I was nudged by my uncle. I looked up and saw that Jackie hadn't touched her plate. He gave me a look that said, 'talk to her you idiot.'

"So, uh, you ready for the summer?" I asked.

"Remove your hat when you're at the table," she said without looking at me. I didn't, and she knew I wasn't going to. My aunt and uncle also knew I wasn't going to. Even my teachers know not to make me take off my hat. I simply pushed my glasses up from the tip of my nose and smiled.

"After dinner, you wanna go for a walk?" I asked with a slightly demanding tone to my voice. It's something my mom does, making a demand with a question. But Jackie paused for a moment and just gave me a blank stare.

"Sure," she finally said. Then she began eating her food. I waited until she was finished, got up, grabbed her by the arm as soon as she put her fork down, and pulled her away from the table. With a wave to my immediate surrogate family, we walked out of the door and headed down the country dirt road that led to the house.

"Alright," I began, "what's your problem?"

"I don't have a problem," she said quickly. "Everybody's trying to act like they don't know what's going on. But I know what's going on."

"What's going on?"

"You really wanna know?"

"That's pretty much why I asked, Jackie."

Jackie stopped in mid-stride and with a sigh said, "Chupacabra."

"Jackie," I said confused, "what the fuck is a chupacabra?"

"Oh, I forgot. You a lil' clean-cut city boy ass nigga. You don't know nothin' bout no lycanthropy."

"Insulting me isn't gonna tell me what a chupalupa is."

"Chupacabra," she corrected me. "Why don't they teach you guys more in city schools? You need to be knowledgeable in this world."

"I am knowledgeable," I told her, "about glocks and war-science though, just like I need to be as a human in this particular world. And rightfully so. I mean, shit, it sounds like we need to buy some silver bullets right the fuck now if you ask me. Is that what you're saying to me? Because Jackie, I got 'em."

I stop talking and fall silent when I catch a blurred image zooming across the field we were standing next to. Both me and my cousin followed its direction with our eyes. After it vanished, we just stood there not saying a damn word to each other for a good two minutes. We were like statues for the moment, like gargoyles trying to comprehend what it was that they had just seen. We still didn't know what we saw, but we were automatically scared because of the topic that just gotten interrupted.

"I wanna go check it out, Matt," she said, heading in the direction of the animal.

"Hell no," I tell her as I begin walking back towards the house.

"Matty," she said in her mischievous voice. That tone meant she had some kind of logic to a troublesome plan.

"If you go home and I'm not with you, my parents will never forgive you if something happens to me. My dad just might kill you." I turn around to face her.

"Think about it," she said, looking me square in the eyes with a half smile on her face, "we'll be finding something sooo rare, dude. This isn't some every day shit. Like, c'mon nattie…name a better way to kick off summer."

I stand there thinking. She had a very enticing point, plus it was also very obvious that she was gonna go regardless of if I went with her or not. In the midst of me making my quick decision. She holds her hand up and says, "But, if you wanna go home and get your piece first, I understand."

Admittedly I frown for a second. I thought she and I were close enough that she'd never need to ask me a question like that. I then shrug and lift my shirt up to my belly to show her the handles of my protection. On my waist, as per usual, were my jet black, .45 caliber twin pistols. And I didn't have them packed with silver bullets, but bullets charged with Universian light will lay out any fucking creature. She nodded her head in agreement of my habits and we headed in the direction of the possible chupacabra.

We kept walking until we heard what sounded like a goat getting murdered. I'd never heard a goat scream before, and possibly still haven't, but if I had to guess on what a goat screaming sounded like then what we heard would be my answer. We followed the sound and ended up at a farm. There were three goats laid out across the grass, obviously dead, and that's when we saw it.

"Jackie, I think that's the chupawumba," I said. She didn't respond to my mispronunciation.

What my cousin and I were looking at was a werewolf looking beast hunched over sucking the blood out of a goat. It was eerily muscular even though it was skinnier than I would've expected a monster to be. The thing that shocked both of us was the long gray Mohawk. It started in the middle of its head and stretched to its tail with the rest of his body covered in thin gray hairs. It was as if he had a barber to style it for him. But then again, nature is the best stylist for plants and animals. Then it hit me, we were standing only twenty feet behind it…openly.

Before I could react the beast turned his head around to face me, revealing a blood covered snout. Staring at us through large emerald eyes, the beast stood upright at a height of 7'4. He began walking towards us slowly. I'm not sure if it was the Human characteristics or the violent green eyes, but Jackie and I stood motionless in shock. They teach us how to defend ourselves from supernatural attacks in school, but werewolves are so uncommon in the world that we never spent much time on what to do against them for real.

The goddamn beast was now dead smack in front of us, breathing all heavy on us, the scent of goat blood all stained on his breath. If someone had been looking at us from afar, they'd have thought that we were just waiting for him to gnaw into one of us. I waited for him to make any sudden moves before I reached for my pistols. But to our surprise, he didn't do anything. Instead, he looked deeply into Jackie's eyes, and I mean real deeply, huffed three times, and turned away from us. Then he just sort of took off for the woods behind him. Just got on all fours, and started to run away. It started off slowly, then picked up speed until we could only hear the bushes rustle when he entered the woods.

"What the fuck?" was all I managed to get out.

"Matty..." Jackie said hyperventilating. She dropped to the ground and I got down too, making sure that I was holding her for comfort. Sadly, it didn't help much.

"You ok?" I asked her.

"No," she said quietly, "Matty, I think I..."

That's when we heard a loud explosion followed by a violent display of lights that set the woods around us on fire. We heard the chupacabra let out a roar, followed by a howl that definitely sounded like it stemmed from excruciating pain. The beams of light continued to shoot out into random directions as the ground shook aggressively beneath us.

I forced my cousin to get to her feet, then I grabbed her by the face and looked her dead in the eyes. With as much seriousness as I could get across without sounding scared for my life, I said to her, "We're getting the fuck out of here. Now."

Without even thinking about it, I pulled my phone out, pulled up the quick menu to open my camera, and I recorded everything as we hauled ass out of there. We ran all the way back to my uncle's house, which was a mile and a half, by the way! Think that mattered to us? Nope! We sprinted the entire way there. There was no way that we were getting caught in that commotion. I kept my body turned to the left, making sure that was the arm catching the battle going on behind us.

We finally saw the house, as well as my aunt and uncle who were both standing on the porch with their jaws dropped. They were watching the commotion going on from afar, the commotion that me and Jackie were running away from. We shot past them without saying a word, they were too in shock to notice though. Gunning straight through the opened front door, we bolted up the stairs and right into Jackie's room.

Sweat drenched our clothes as we laid on her hardwood floor, gasping for air and sore in the limbs. The camera on my iPhone was still recording when I held it to my face, making sure I had the selfie camera flipped on. Looking Straight at my phone, I straight up said, "Holy shit. Holy shit balls and mackrels. We just found a chupacabra... then it got killed in a Universian battle man! What kinda shit is that?!"

"Turn that damn thing off, Matty!" Jackie yells at me. I swiftly end the recording and sit up to look at her. "We don't know that!"

"Yo, this is the wildest night of my life," I confess to her.

Still gasping for air, she looks up at me and nods her head with closed eyes. She held up her fist, to which I proudly give a bump to with my own. The fight between the hypernaturals was still going strong just two miles from my family's home. We couldn't see the actual fight, but we could see lights and hear the destruction that they were causing in the woods. How they were managing to keep it contained to that one particular area was impressive though, can't lie.

"We just saw some fucking Universians," I said in excitement.

"No," she said through deep breathes. "We saw a Universian battle. We're still seeing a Universian battle. But we also saw a chupacabra. Told you it was real."

"Yeah you were right," I admit to her.

I lay back down on the hardwood floor, my head next to hers. "I guess no one should be surprised by anything at this point. Makes you look at old fables a little bit differently, huh?"

"It's just crazy though," Jackie said aloud. Finally, she sat up. "When I was looking at that monster, looking into his eyes I felt like I knew him."

I look up at her in amusement and ask her, "What do you mean exactly?"

"I think it's mortal," she tells me, "to some degree, anyways. And I definitely know him...I think I know him very well."

I sit up and look at her in confusion. I felt like I knew what she meant by that, but I wasn't sure. But from the way that her voice trailed off as she thought about the chupacabra we'd seen, I could tell that if that thing was mortal she'd definitely been banging its humanoid form at some point.

As we sit on my cousin's bedroom floor and I come to my realization, me and Jackie both start laughing. It was weird. I guess after surviving something like that, that was our best reaction. Our giggles began to die down when we noticed the rumbling from the Earthers and the Lighters had stopped, and the white lights we had been seeing suddenly stopped too. I'm not sure if we were in shock or bedazzled, but we stood up when purple lights began flashing from where the battle had been. The rays of violet lit up the entire area, easily making my cousin's room look like one of Prince's dreams. After about twenty seconds, the purple lights also stopped. The rumbling that had accompanied the violet light show had ceased. It just became very quiet. No birds chirping, no crickets cricketing, just silence.

I looked at Jackie, thinking that maybe she knew something that I didn't. She looked back at me, and tucked some of her hair behind her left ear.

"No idea what that was," she told me bluntly. "But damn. That's some powerful stuff."

IF FOUND PLEASE RETURN TO:

Luna

chapter three

6/26/2022

A Page From Luna's Journal

I find myself playing around with the food on my tray. I usually love the lasagna that the cafeteria serves. I mean, it's kind of hard to mess up a dish when you have numerous spells to cook up perfect recipes. But on this particular day...on this day I was just sooo not in the mood for it. I was trying to ignore the fact that in the back of my mind, something in the universe felt off.

I hadn't washed my hair in two weeks so it was looking more brown than black, at least to me. Allison sat across from me, reading an article on her phone about the Shadow Society's New York governor's so-called scandal with that young hot Korean woman that worked in his office. I wondered why people would even care that an unwed governor would bang his single, and in my opinion stunningly attractive, office secretary. I mean, it's not like he's a pastor or anything. He's a famous male politician. Then again, I'm also a bit biased towards the girl because, you know, I'm Korean too.

"Luna," Allison says to me, breaking my concentration. "Are you okay? You haven't touched your food."

"Not hungry," I say, still twirling my fork on a piece of cheese. I can tell that it's cooling down, so I blow on it to heat it up some more. One of my favorite spells to do.

"Well, that doesn't make any sense," she tells me. "You're always hungry. Is something bothering you?"

I didn't really know how to answer that. Truth is, I am always hungry. But something actually was bothering me, I just had no clue as to what. Since nothing had presented itself as a problem yet, I simply said to my best friend, "It's nothing."

Allison makes a face that lets me know she doesn't really believe what I'm telling her. She turns her blue cap backwards so that her short blonde hair is sticking out of the hole at the top. Then she decides to quickly switch the topic from my downside attitude to something more interesting. In an instant, her newspaper transforms into a flyer. It's a kid dressed in all black holding up an odd hand sign and what looked like a book of spells in the other hand. Behind him was a wall of speakers

with what looked like a golden throne in the dead center. A hood is pulled over the guy's head so low that only the bottom half of his face was showing. Had to admit, it was a pretty cool flyer. But what really stood out to me was the name of the headlining act.

"Oh! Hell yeah," I say excitedly. For some strange reason, I knew exactly which song she was referring to. It had me hooked instantly. It was some raspy-voiced kid singing about how he'd "cast a spell on that hoe." It took my heart away instantly. "So I'm guessing he's the guy that made it," I say to her, throwing just a wee bit of obnoxiousness on my guess.

As a huge hip-hop fanatic myself, I couldn't help but notice how good the guy was at actually rapping. It didn't make me think too much, but he still made sense. And, he had a flow that really made me wanna dance, but also listen to him. Not only that, but he was making some really clever witchcraft references too. So, of course, I thought it was not only interesting, but relatable for someone like myself. A witch. The only reason that we didn't ask the Duber driver for the artist's name was because he kept staring at Allison's perky c-cups all pervy, and he was much older than our tender ages of seventeen. But the song still ended up getting stuck in my head for a few days after that.

"Yep. He's having a show in Harlem tonight," Allison excitedly informs me. "We're definitely going."

I think about it briefly, very briefly, and say, "I don't know if I want to go off the strength of one song. I need to hear more."

"Well I'm sure we could find his Soundcloud link in a hot second," Allison said in her smart-alecky tone. "I mean, we know his name now."

I always find it so pleasantly annoying when Allison's right. But once again, she made a good point. This guy's song was really good and it never ever hurts to check out a few songs from a new artist. Right?

"Ehh, okay," I tell her. "I'll check his lil' repertoire out tonight. I'll let you know what I think." Then lunch ends and we head to our next class.

Our school, Loretti's Collegiate Academy For the Strong & Powerful, has been around for 500 years now. It's like a private elite college for witches and warlocks, but it also doubles as a training ground for Wiccan warriors. I like the school most days, but then I also hate it because of all the damn rules; especially now. My people had been having an overly drawn out beef against the goblins at one point. Sorry, I meant Eartians. But in 2004, with no talks of treaty or surrender from either side, we stopped fighting each other all together. Next we all just sort of went into pseudo-hiding. And by, "we all," I mean Elves, Humans, and Eartians too. For the first time in hundreds of years, supernatural creatures are keeping a low profile in society. Me personally, I think it's because of the Universian War.

It's just a theory of mine, but I believe that one of us got in their way during one of their so-called "secret" battles. And I think some of our best people were slaughtered in the process. Not just on our side either, but probably the Eartians too. Surely enough, our superiors never talk about what's really going on, so we're all just left to assume the worst. But it can't be a coincidence that this all started when the Universians began their civil war. I mean, I'll just be real, the hypernaturals are sort of like tiny gods walking among us. They could probably destroy the planet as we know it...if they ever really wanted to, of course.

Out of all of the supernatural creatures, Wiccans are the ones who look the most Human. Yet, on the mortal vibrational scale, Wiccans come second, right after the pacifist Elfen people. In the past, my people were notorious for abusing our powers, often attacking the magically weaker Humans and Eartians for the fun of it. Because of this, we can only interact with the Human world during the evenings for six hours max while enrolled in school. It used to be ten, but I guess they feel like there's still some leeway because we get full Saturdays. I know that they just don't want us picking a fight with a Universian in a grocery store, I guess. But regardless, curfews suck.

I sometimes envy the hypernaturals, because I know for a fact that a good amount of both Earthers and Lighters exist amongst Humans and Eartians outside of their respective safe haven cities. But at the same time though, interacting with naturals is really weird for me. Humans and Eartians are boring, yo. I mean, I guess it's kind of cool that Eartians have roots in Mars, but that's about it. They were enslaved by Wiccans for like a hundred years though, so that also makes it weird. Besides, elves are originally from another planet too. So once again, the Mars thing isn't impressive. And supernaturally powered humans are so scarce it's genuinely sad. They're still tough, ruthless creatures though. So I guess if I'm being honest with myself, I just hate being told to censor myself. I know I can't say all of this out loud around other sentients.

As I'm sitting in my fourth period class, Animal Communications 111, one of the school's superintendents knocks on our classroom door. I wouldn't have paid any attention to it any other day, but today I was the one she asked to have excused from class.

I was genuinely concerned on my walk to the High Risen Grand Master's office. My escort didn't say anything to me the entire time we were heading there. Was I in some sort of trouble? I'd surely watched some porn a few days prior, and that's definitely restricted on school grounds, but I've got a good proxy. Well, at least so I thought. Plus everyone knows the elders don't really know how to use computers, and there ain't a spell for a proxy code but I knew if they found out I was surely screwed. No pun intended.

Finally we get to the office. The High Risen Grand Master of the school, or Grand Master for short, was a very tiny blue-eyed lady named Helga Loretti. A beautiful older woman with creamy caramel colored skin from her mixed Nigerian and Iranian heritage, Mrs. Loretti's power is feared by all underground creatures across the entire globe. She may be tiny in stature, but her magical abilities are almost immeasurable. Needless to say, there was no way in hell I was about talk out of term. She sat behind her desk silently, staring at a sheet of paper. I stood there waiting for her to say something. She remained silent for a while, so I did

41

the same. Slowly, she shows me the paper that she'd been staring at. It's the flyer Allison had shown me of that rapper, the artist whose show we were going to see.

"Ms. Luna Ling," she says to me with what felt like the warmest of smiles. A stream of light shone through the purple drapes, and shed light on her face, illuminating her matching purple eyes. Glimmers flashed from the diamond and emerald studded necklace she wore so elegantly around her neck. Mrs. Loretti's head of long, flowing, knotty grey hair even seemed to glisten a bit in the light. Why is she so damn perfect at age 60?

"Hello there," she said to me with that perfect white smile of hers. "It's so very nice to see you today."

"Hi, Mrs. Loretti," I replied.
"Warlock the MC," she says with a smile, the wrinkles at the corners of her violet eyes deepening a bit. "That's quite the stage name for a rapper. Have you listened to any of his music?"
"No," I say quickly. "Well, just one song."
I'm still not sure if I'm in trouble at this point, so I'm still a tad bit anxious.

"You can relax sweetie," Mrs. Loretti says to me assuringly. "You're not in any trouble."

I let out a super loud sigh of relief. Mrs. Loretti waved her emerald covered left hand, and a chair flew rapidly from the right side of the wall and skidded directly behind me, hitting the back of my knees with just the right amount of force so that my knees painlessly buckle and I involuntarily find myself sitting down. The Grand Master's smile began to fade away slowly. Her smile dropping the way it did, it made me notice that the room was a lot creepier than I remembered it being last year. Her office environment was something determined by her smile. I wonder if that's intentional or not.
Anyways, I wasn't able to hold in the question that was eating at me since I was summoned to Mrs. Loretti's office. So in my calmest, sweetest, most innocent voice that I use on my mother, I

asked her, "Why am I here?"

"This young man," she says, showing me the flyer once again, "this, Warlock the MC. I want you to go to his show tonight, just as you and Allison were planning to do. But it's very essential that you bring him back here."

"Um, why?" I ask through my confusion. I was mostly wondering how she knew Allison and I were planning on going to his show in the first place. But I was just as curious as to why she wanted us to go retrieve him.

"Because it's not just a stage name," Mrs. Loretti told me, "he's truly a warlock. And now, we need for him to come home."

"But Grand Master," I say, "Wiccans don't have to attend a school in the Shadow Society if they choose not to, so long as they don't cause any major disturbances in the outside world. Like, that's definitely a known fact. And I'm not questioning your motives, but I'm pretty sure his career has caused him to not need to go to school at the moment. Apparently, he's got a lot of fans already and I just didn't know. Which is a thing these days. So I'm trying to understand why, as you say, he needs to come here?"

Mrs. Loretti let out a huge sigh. She was making it pretty evident that she wasn't all that comfortable with talking to me about whatever it was that she was getting ready to say. But she needed my help, so she had to tell me something.

"All I can tell you right now," she began with a sigh, "is that goddamn boy is very, very important to us. All of us. Have you discovered his real name yet?"

I shake my head in response to signal, 'no.'
"He doesn't have a Wikipedia page yet," I tell her.

"That's probably because he doesn't want one." She paused before saying his name aloud, "Solomon Allura."
I'm not exaggerating when I say that I truly believe I felt my heart stop beating for a moment. A warlock with the last name Allura? I knew instantly what this had to mean.
"You mean to tell me that he's Mvula Allura's son?" I ask almost rhetorically.

"No," she says. "He's her grandchild."
"Wow. Are you sure?"
"Completely positive," she says. "That sign he's holding up with his right hand, that's a warrior sign from his father's side of the family."
I lean back in my chair a little bit in disbelief. I was hearing that an Allura family member was still alive. Not only that, but he was rapping. Why would he be out in the open like that?
"We've been searching for him for the past three months," Mrs. Loretti continued, "ever since his powers began peaking. They still happen to be developing, actually. But he's already long surpassed even the most powerful senior here."

"Really? He's stronger than Shakk? What the..." I begin stammering over my words from the information I'm being told. "But, how? How old is he?

"About sixteen or seventeen," she told me. "Around your age, for sure."

"No way! He's still peaking?"

"Yes, and will be for a while, child. It's a very, very long, long story," she said raising her left hand and she shaking her head aggressively. It made me realize it actually was a dramatically long story.

She continued, "Here's what you need to know, his mother thought it'd be best to keep him hidden. Unfortunately for her, that's not going to work anymore. We need him here."

"Okay, so why are you telling me this?"

Mrs. Loretti smiled at me, and I lie to you not, that was the first time in my entire life that I've ever felt special. It was like I was being chosen for something bigger than myself. And I knew this simply from the smile that she gave me.

"All you need to know, Luna," she said looking me directly in the eye, "is that you're the right match for this job. Besides, it's apparent that he wants to be found. Tonight, I want you and Allison to go to that concert and bring Solomon home. His true home. Here. Alive, please. Can you do that?"

"Yeah," I tell her. "Hell yeah! I mean...yes ma'm. Should I not tell Allison about this?"

"She's being informed of this as we speak," she assured me. "You both will be on one accord.Skip your last class today, as I've already had you both excused, research his music, and then go to the show tonight."

After leaving Mrs. Loretti's office, I found myself sitting with Allison in my room for the next three hours listening to Solomon's music. I was shocked. Mainly because it was really, really good! And with knowing his background, I started to question if he'd learned some kind of spell to make people fall in love with his music. Allison and I listened to his first two mixtapes as we showered, I made sure to thoroughly wash my hair. As we were getting dressed, I put his most recent EP on repeat until we left for the show. While we were getting ready, I couldn't help but to bring up what was eating at my mind.

"Do you think he's our next High Risen?"

I asked Allison as I pushed my titties into a more comfortable position to go with the black halter top I had just thrown over my head.

"Ya know, I really don't know, Luna," Allison answered quickly, almost as if she'd been wondering the same thing. A little bit more excitedly she said, "I was thinking about that when Mrs. Loretti told you the whole thing about how he's still in the beginning process of his peak. Like, he's just starting that process, but he'll still be the strongest person here when he arrives. That's like having double d cups and an exquisite, acne free face as soon as you start puberty."

"That's not necessarily a good thing," I say to her strongly. "That could make a girl a target."

"My point exactly. His powers are big tits, the music the pretty face, and now he's our target."

"Wait," I say to her, "How's his music the pretty face?"

"If his music was terrible, Loretti would've had a much harder time finding him."

I didn't have to think about it too long. We weren't going on some underground boat trip across the Atlantic to find the strongest Wiccan we've heard about in fifty years hidden in a cave somewhere. There were no minions to get past, no guardians around him. The dude was doing a rap show in Brooklyn because people like his music filled with shit-talking Wiccan spell references. All we had to do to find him was look pretty at a concert. Easy. All because his pretty faced music made it that way.

"Yeah," I say as I shrug in agreement. "you're right. You always are. But his family has been exiled for a half a century now. Is his power really getting so strong that Loretti wants him at the school? Like, really? Wouldn't she want to stay away from him?"

"You think she's lying about how strong he really is?"

"No," I say as I sit on the bed, right next to the speaker, "I I think he's as strong as she says. But I think that something's coming that's probably even scarier than him. I think Loretti wants to be prepared for it. I think she wants a weapon for the Wiccans."

I close my eyes and turn the music up, letting the exiled boy's voice fill my ears until I felt like I was look-ing at him. I honestly don't know if the Solomon situation concerns me, or turns me on. I think it's a bit of both. Crazy thing is though, we can't find any pictures of his actual face online anywhere. Maybe it's all of the hype around him. Maybe it's how his singing voice sounds. But whatever it was, I definitely feel drawn to him. Hopefully he's cute, but most importantly nice. Loretti's husband exiled the Allura's personally, he might not take so kindly to us trying to entice him to come back to her school with us. Okay, well Allison is finally finished getting dressed now, so I think I'll end off here for today. I just needed to get this all down on paper one last time. Just in case, you know, this dude kills us on the spot or something.

But it's just now really dawning on me. If this boy is really as strong as Grand Master Loretti says he is, then we also can't be the only ones looking for him...

CHAPTER FOUR

THE WEDDING TOAST

The reception was jam-packed with family and friends from all over the country and time. Some people hadn't been seen in years and others had managed to stay around rather consistently. Nevertheless, all was well as smiles flowed through tears in this happy and humble beginning which stemmed from the union of a strong, well respected man and his strong, well respected new wife.

The best man, who was the step-brother and best friend of the groom, marched in with a beautiful bridesmaid, who also happened to be his wife. Laughing and moving energetically, they made their way to their seats. When the bride and groom walked in, the uproar of applause was immense. It was obvious that this young couple, so full of potential, truly loved each other down to the very chambers of their hearts. The groom smiled adoringly at his new wife, happier than he'd ever been in his life and his brother knew this more than anyone. As dinner was beginning to be served, the best man's wife looked at him with childlike curiosity. Noticing the look of worry that had rushed his face she asked him, "What's wrong, baby?"

The best man looked from side to side and replied, "I don't know what I'm going to say for the toast."

"Oh sweetie," she said rubbing his back, "you'll be fine. Why are you nervous? The war won't find us here, there's literally nothing to worry about. If you speak from the heart you'll do just fine."

"If I speak from the inside, the guests will just hear my stomach growlin' like a muh-fucker, babe," he said with a slight chuckle.

His wife giggled, flashing hazel eyes from a caramel skinned face over her silk white face mask and replied, "Well then speak from the heart."

Before he could reply, he saw the groom making a face that read, 'okay, it's time for you to start talking now.' He comprehended the expression on his brother's face and stood to his feet with his glass raised. A server had come over to bring him a microphone, then he took a deep breath.

"Can I have everyone's attention, please," he said in an obnoxiously deep voice. All guests stopped and did as such. "Thanks. Now, everyone knows that today's is my brother's special day and as the best man it's my job to make a special toast. Now I don't want to make this about me in any way-"

"Then don't!" shouted his uncle humorously, getting a laugh from everyone.

"Watch yourself old man," he replied back, receiving another laugh. He then continued with, "As most of you all know, the wonderful groom here and I are step-brothers. But blood couldn't make us any closer. The story of how we became close describes just how amazing my brother truly is." He paused to take a deep breath then continued.

"I was about six years old when my father began beating my mother," he said, "and eight years old when my mother built up the courage to take me and leave. We had no money, lived in a rough neighborhood...it was tough. I remember she used to just cry and cry all of the time, and seeing her that sad hurt. So one day, I decided that after school that I was going to...blow my brains out with the pistol my mom kept under her mattress. I was about ten or so."

Everyone gasped at their tables, apparently shocked by what they'd just heard. The best man looked at his own wife, who didn't know this particular story about her husband. He then continued. "On the day I was going to end my short life, I was on my way home from school when this happy go lucky kid on a red and green bicycle runs into me and knocks my books out of my hand. He looks at me and says, 'Sorry, let me get that for you.'" The guests laughed at the tiny voice he used to impersonate his younger brother.

"Now he didn't just pick the books up and go on about his way, he carried my books home for me and let me ride his bike, or attempt to since I didn't know how. He stayed with me for two and a half hours teaching me how to ride a bicycle and I learned. So now the boy who was going to selfishly take his own life, had someone that he could learn from. We started hanging out every day after that and we were inseparable. We still are, as you can see. But one day he's at my house and he sees my mother crying. Now his mother passed away when he was five, so he knows pain...but he walks up to her, grabs her hand and tells her, 'Are you lonely? It's okay. I think I can help you fix that.'"

The best man stopped and looked at his brother, seeing the tears beginning to form in his eyes as he remembered that day. He quickly looked away to avoid having his emotions take hold of him before he finished the story. Feeling how everyone was anticipating what he would say next, he continued on.

"So he goes home, and he tells his father, who is still one of the only men I'll ever say I love, that he should go on a date with my 'really hot mom.' Like really, who says that?" He paused for a moment as laughter came his way. "But he listened to his son, and they fell in love. After two years of dating, they got married. Let me tell you, there's nothing more exciting to two little boys who are best friends then find out that they're going to be brothers."

There was a cheer after these words were spoken, but it soon died down. They wanted to hear more to this heartfelt backstory. The best man smiled and said, "In my life, I avoided death by my own hand. I've kept a loving mother, who rarely cries now, might I add. I've gained a man worthy enough to call my father. But what's most special to me, is that I gained a brother in all of this first. And it all comes from a happy go lucky kid who ran into me on his red and green bicycle one day. Had it not been for that, I wouldn't be here right now to see such a beautiful couple start their journey of taking on the world together. I do believe in happiness, and I do believe in fate, and it's all because of my brother. To the newlyweds."

The best man raised his glass, as did everyone else in the room of the reception. He looked to his parents, who both had tears running down their faces, and soon he felt his brother hugging him tightly as his wife held his hand. He looked at the groom and smiled warmly, glad to have been able to make his brother's special day all the more special. With a wink and a warm smile, the best man asked his wife, "So was that a good toast?"

The groom then gently raised his right hand, causing a few pieces of wooden floor tile to crumble. Then, a large mound of soil pushed up from the hole in the middle of the dining hall floor. Next, the bride poked her index finger in the direction of the miniature soil hill. Lo and behold, grass, branches, and leaves rapidly grew as freed dirt fell back down to the roots. In mere seconds, large pink roses began blossoming in full until a four-foot rose bush stood proudly in the middle of the wedding reception. Eather weddings truly are the most beautiful.

CHAPTER FIVE

SOLOMON ALLURA

I remember backstage being a fucking mess. My manager, Paulie Girl, was cursing out a food attendant because she had brought us peanut M&M's instead of peanut butter ones. I was sitting back twirling with one of my go-to braids as I watched my ex-girlfriend roll tree up with the girl that I'd been getting to know more recently. Much to my surprise, they were getting along awesomely. Darius, my DJ, and Conway, my bassist, were having a debate about if General Rocket was the one who actually brought back NY rap or not. I wasn't really paying attention to that though, I was wondering where Lemon was. He had told me that he was getting his drum kit worked on, which is believable because electronic drum kits can be tricky. But personally, I think he went to go see one of the girl's we met out in Jersey the other day. I loved my outfit today, too. We

wore all black for the entire tour, mainly because it was the easiest way to look like a unit. I was wearing a new pair of stylishly ripped black skinny jeans, a tight fit black hoodie, a black leather jacket, and a black t-shirt with a picture of Tony Flow looking like Mona Lisa (he's kinda my role model in life). But I was hella excited about the gold chain I'd just gotten. No one knew, but the charm of it is an old Egyptian Coptic Cross made out of rubies that I stole from a museum during our stop in DC. Thank God for camera illusory spells, right? And tonight, my hair was freshly braided, the last piece of my neck tattoo had just healed up and I had the new Adiddons on my feet. I was fly as hell for the last tour stop, boyyyy!!!

My ex finished up with what she was doing and was just beginning to light up when Lemon finally burst through doing dry heaves with a humongous smile on his face. We all looked up to see what he was going to say, especially after that dramatic entrance he'd just given.

"Bro," he said loudly. "It's super packed out there!"

"I told you we'd sell this show out!" Paulie started yelling at us. "I told you." She got me so excited that I jumped up and started dapping everyone up. This was my first time headlining a tour and the whole thing was sold out. We had taken a small bet to see if we'd be able to sell out all of the tickets in NY. Thank God she even took off her nerdy wireframes and shouted a loud 'woo!'

I love Paulie Girl, yo. She's a butch lesbian girl who always keeps her hair pulled back into a ponytail braid. Somehow she kinda dresses like a young boy band member because she feels weird about her own big booty. Paulie really did fit in with us pretty well, mainly because she liked cracking jokes. The minute she heard my music though, she told me real sternly that she was my manager. I wasn't really thinking she was serious about it until she texted me and told me that I was opening up for Tae Free. Even then I didn't believe her until I saw the flyers and heard my name on the radio for it.

Now, we had just completed my first North American tour. We sold out every single fucking city we played in. This was a dream come true for me. I was ready as fuck to play a sold-out show to my hometown. We went outside to the stage, where we instantly heard people chanting "Warlock!! Warlock!! Warlock!!" over, and over, and over again. I'd been performing in New York for three years straight, just trying to get my name heard. My music was good, and I was slowly picking up steam, but it wasn't at the pace that I really wanted it to be. So when I came across a music spell at this old vintage boutique shop down in Virginia, I used it for my benefit. Apparently, the last time somebody used the spell, a whole town danced until they died. That wasn't my intent with it at all.

Magic's like salt, ya know? Too much will kill the food. But use just the right amount, and you've got the base for possible perfect flavor. Intent, tone, confidence, projection, these are all just some of the extra seasonings that go into a spell being cast. How much you put in it determines how strong your spell is. My grandma, a powerful ass Cajun witch, used to call the strength of a spell it's "flavor." And being that I just sold out Terminal 5 for the last show on my tour in NY, I know grandma would be proud of all the seasonings I've been putting into this gumbo pot that I call my music career.

I mean, the feeling tonight was unexplainable. We hit the stage, and the crowd was beyond lit, on some real shit. I mean, they were screaming as wildly as I could've ever dreamed. It felt like something out of a movie. I grabbed the microphone with my right hand and held my middle finger up with my left. The crowd began screaming louder and all copied my gesture.

"Darius!" I yelled out. "Drop the beat!!"

The beginning synths to my song Run For The Mountains began to play. I turned to the crowd, the bass-line bouncing rhythmically at a steady half-time pace in the key of F. I've now got six bars until my first verse starts. I'm getting hyped up and I turn. I jump up and down to the rhythm and begin engaging the crowd.

"Mosh pit!" I scream and demand. "I wanna see a fucking mosh pit! Right now, dammit!"

The mosh pit begins to open and the first few people hop into the middle. I'm about to say the first lyric when I see a girl in the crowd that completely catches me off guard. It's an Asian chick with long, thick, jet black hair with all types of magical energy floating around her. The blonde haired girl beside her had magic coursing through her little Wiccan veins too, but it wasn't quite as strong as first girl I saw. The way that they were looking at me didn't sit well with me. I mean, the blonde haired chick was pretty excited about the show, but the girl I was looking at didn't seem like she came to have fun. There was a weird look of determination in her eyes. I couldn't take my eyes off of them. Two measures before I was supposed to start rapping, I wave my hand and recite in my mind the time spell that my grandma taught me as a boy. It's "forbidden," apparently, but I still use it anyways.

Everyone in the room was frozen still, including my bandmates. The only people that could move were me and the two Wiccan girls in the crowd that I'd excluded from my spell. For the next fifteen minutes, we would exist in a bubble outside of the third dimension, which most people would perceive to be time. And since I was the one who'd casted the spell, everything was sure to be on my terms. I wasn't surprised at the fact that they only looked semi-surprised that I'd used a time stopping spell. I guess if they had the balls to come at me, makes sense they'd have done some research on me. I mean, I know I'm not just a national musician now. I'm also a third-generation exiled Wiccan in the eyes of the shadow law and I've been using magic to get ahead in my career. But trust me, I won't ever hiding from anybody.

Supernatural lifeforms, the Elves and the Wiccans, such as myself, we can all feel how powerful another creature is. The only creatures we can't seem to do this with are the Universians. They aren't natural or supernatural creatures, they're hypernaturals.

They're more powerful than us...usually. But regardless, most magical creatures have been keeping a low profile until the war between the Lighters and the Earthers really dies down, ya know?

So I hop off the stage and begin walking through all of the people in the unmoving crowd until I make my way to the center of the fifth row. I wanted to look these two girls dead in their eyes before I decided on whether or not I would turn them into a piles of pearls to give to my grandma, or let them enjoy my show. Either way, I was gonna finish my show.

"You two know who I really am, I see," I said to them directly. Won't no need to ask any rhetorical shit.

"Yeah," the blonde girl said with a small quiver in her voice. She was a deep feeler, the outright strength of my magic was disrupting her aura like pollen to a humans nose. It was quite literally making her body uncomfortable, which made sense on a few levels in this case.

She then said, "You're an Allura, right? Solomon?"

I didn't say anything. Instead, I asked the leader between the two of them, the Asian girl, what her name was.

"Luna," she said with a commendable amount of confidence. She pointed her thumb at her friend and said, "My friend is Allison. You'll have to excuse her, she's a feeler."

"Figured. So, why are you guys here exactly?" I gave them with my best fake smile. "I bet that you two go to Loretti's School, don't you? Who's running the show now? Helga, right?"

"She says that it's time that you return home," Luna told me. "She believes that some very dangerous people are looking for you and she just wants to make sure that you're safe."

"Did she tell you to apologize on her and her family's behalf for exiling my grandmother and the rest of my family thirty years ago?" I asked them.

"No," Luna responded, "unfortunately, she did not."

She seemed genuinely sympathetic, I'll give her that. But it wasn't enough for me to go with them. Honestly, I asked them that already knowing that Helga Loretti would never apologize for any of the shit that's happened to my family in the last few decades.

"I appreciate the gesture," I tell her sarcastically before saying, "but sweetie, dangerous people are always after me. Trust me, I can take care of my own damn self. Get the fuck outta here. Or stay and watch the show. Your choice."

I was pissed at the fact that she even sent people to communicate with me. I didn't give a damn if it was a warning or not. Like I said, I ain't hidin'. She had to know that I could've really hurt these girls in ways she can't even fathom. Was she losing her marbles in her new position? Stress maybe? Or maybe she needed me for something else. Perhaps she was hoping I'd stand a chance fighting a Universian...which she'd be right about. But that would also mean that she knows one of my biggest secrets.

But ultimately I know she knew that I wouldn't kill her messengers. It went against my family's code. I couldn't just destroy two pretty young girls sent to give a message. We all knew that they couldn't take me by force, they weren't anywhere near strong enough. For a moment, the three of us were just staring at each other, though I still had trouble taking my eyes off of Luna. She was fucking gorgeous to me. "Well look," I begin to tell them as I turn around to

get back on stage, "if people are looking for me, I ain't hidin'. You two, tell Mrs. Loretti that I said, 'eat a dick'."

I turn around to hop my black ass back on stage so that I can resume time and continue on with my show. I'm still in the crowd facing my still frozen-in-time bandmates when I felt this surge of energy generating from behind me. I turn around to see Luna's hands covered with glowing sparkling rose colored energy, and her palms are actually pointed towards me. She had a smile on her face. I honestly remember thinking to myself, 'Is this bitch crazy?' I try not to laugh from looking at her. And even though the look on her face was playful, the look in her eyes were full of determination. Her friend Allison, did not look determined. Worried was a better word. She definitely knew that Luna was in over her head. But in good Allura fashion, I shrug and show her something that I know for a fact most Wiccans you'll come across wouldn't know about.

With a smile on my face, I held up a small orb of black matter energy, sparkling with little tiny lights dancing all around it. I watch in amusement as their faces go blank with shock from the fact that I could not only harness this type of magic, but that I could generate it so effortlessly. Her pink colored magical sparks vanished quickly, thanks to my response. She straightened up and sighed. Then she chuckled.

"That was just small for you, huh?" She said to me. "Jesus. What the fuck have you had to do to become so powerful, yet remain a complete asshole? Huh, dude?"

That's when I also noticed a curvy elf girl wearing a white dress with emeralds decorating her all over. She was floating in the air behind them. Her power was faint, but only because she wasn't really there, ya know. But there was seriously something odd about her energy. Powerful. I'd been with a few elf girls that kind of looked like this one before. You know brown skin with the face of a middle eastern girl. But what really stood out to me was the kinky auburn colored hair that naturally flowed down to her shoulders. The pointy tips of her ears peeked out of her hair like shy squirrels saying hi from in the bushes. Those emerald green eyes definitely stood out to me, glowing and pulsating at a steady four count pace as brightly as the actual emerald in the middle of her dress. Did I mention that I could see through her? She was translucent! I remember thinking that if these girls had brought along a green ghost elf chick, they were really trying everything they could to get me to go back with them.

"So was she supposed to be your backup plan in this?" I asked them, pointing to the elf behind them. Both girls turned around and stared far longer than they should have. I knew instantly that all they could see was the time frozen crowd around them. They kept looking around before turning back at me in confusion.

"Dude, who are you talking about?" Luna asked me. "Nobody's there."

The reason that this bothered me was because I knew there was very blatantly somebody there. I immediately figured this elf girl was indeed using astral projection but was also using a spell so that only I could see her.

Powerful magic, for sure. I knew if I was the only one who could see her, there was some serious intent here. Ironically enough,

I had two chicks in the crowd telling me that people were looking for me, so I figured I'd give her a chance to speak with me. I wave my right hand once more, this time freezing Luna and Allison along with everyone else in the room. They'd be frozen for the remaining eight minutes I had left on the spell.

Sensing that we were now alone, the translucent elf girl casually floated towards me, arms folded, a small smile across her thin face. The projection of her looked at me square in the eye, and she said, "You feel just as powerful as your father."

"I still might have a long way to go for that," I tell her. "So, what's up? You gon' tell me who you are?"

"You know who I am," she told me. She began floating in circles around me, which made me uneasy. I didn't know her but judging from her response, I figured maybe another version of myself did. A future version, most likely. From following her movements, I knew there wasn't much she could do to harm me in her current state even if she really wanted to.

She then said to me, "You know I'm here to show you the future, right?"

"Figured, but why? And who are you? I'm really just tryna finish this show, yo. Can we get on with this shit?"

"I don't have that much time. We think that you can be the one to stop it, but you could also be the one who allows it to happen. You HAVE to go to the school. That's how you stop it."

"You're speaking in riddles baby," I tell her. "Speak straightfor-wardly, please."

They say that actions speak louder than words. I never knew how true that was until that day. The Elf descended to become eye level with me. Then she placed her hands on my ears, where I felt tingles of what felt like electricity prickling from her fingertips. She exhaled, letting a mint green colored, mint scented cloud of smoke escape from her mouth. Fearlessly, I inhaled it. Then everything went black.

Sight flickered back into my eyes and everything became clear again. I was on another stage, but I quickly realized that I was looking over a burning forest as I stood on top of what seemed to be a Mayan pyramid. The sky was a bright blue and the sun, for some reason, now had a large silver ring around it. But there were thousands upon thousands of people in a large crowd in front of me screaming in excitement. Their screams were making me feel high for some reason.

Behind me was my DJ, my bassist, and my electro-drummer. I noticed that I had a new keyboardist. An Elf! Light brown complexion dude with cornrows. Here, I know that I know him, but I also know that I haven't met him *yet*! Still hovering above the crowd, I see the Elf girl smiling at me with flashing emerald colored eyes.

"Spit!" Darius yelled out to me. "Spit somethin'! Sing, fool! Start the damn show!"

The beat drops and the crowd goes crazy. I stand in the middle of the stage, letting my ears soak up the roaring sounds of what felt like well over ten thousand beautiful souls. I saw Elves, Wiccans, Eartians, and Humans, ranging from all skin shades of sand and wood, began singing along to my words. Even in the midst of a fire, all of the creatures of Earth had finally found a way to rejoice and put aside all of our differences for the love of music. And much to my delight, I couldn't get a read on any Universians.

Right when I begin to feel the satisfaction of unity, I feel an energy that feels more massive than anything I've ever felt. I knew it was the power of a person, but it felt like it was coming from the sun. But it also felt like it was coming from me. Over the sound of the pounding music, we all hear a loud crashing sound. This caused me, my band, and the entire audience to look around at the sky in confusion. I notice three white pyramid shaped ships zoom upward into the atmosphere. Then, there was a powerful beam of reddish-orange light that shot out from the sun itself, turning the entire crowd into ashes in a matter of mere seconds. The powerful blast stopped just inches in front of my face. For the first time in a long time I stood there paralyzed in fear, staring at that bright, orange colored light.

"If you want to stop this," the pretty Elfin girl spirit projection said to me, "then sing to her. Sing to Luna. Then, go home."

Then the blast resumes, finally makes its way to the stage, preparing to eat me and the rest of my band. I smile and embrace it. This is true power.

I hear the word "Warlock" being shouted over and over again. When I came to, again, I found that I was walking onstage with my band as the crowd shouted in excitement. I quickly realize that somebody set time back ten minutes, and that's super forbidden. Why was someone sending me elf visions? I knew I needed answers. So I did what I felt like my dad would've done in my shoes. I stop time again and hop off stage once more, rushing over to where I knew I'd see Luna and Allison.

"Luna. Allison," I call to them before they have a chance to respond to the fact that, to them, time has been frozen around them for only the first time. "Loretti sent you two to get me, right?"

"Uhhh," was all a quivering Allison managed to say.

"Yes," Luna said quickly, struggling to keep her composure. She reached out her hand for a gestured shake. "I don't know how you knew our names, but you seem to know time spells so I guess I'm not that surprised. Loretti wanted us to tell you-"

"Yeah, yeah, yeah," I said cutting her off quickly. "Look, stick around after the show tonight, okay? I've got questions for Helga and I need you two to take me to her. So, I'll be returning to Loretti's school with y'all after the show. I'm Solomon by the way. Nice to meet you two."

Caught in an emotional mixture of shock and excitement, both Luna and Allison had trouble hiding their feelings of accomplishment. I didn't tease or poke fun at them for it though, I simply turned around and rushed back onstage. I grabbed the microphone, just as I'd done a few minutes prior, and snapped my fingers so that time could resume. Instantly, my ears are met with the roaring screams of five hundred fans. With my microphone in my right hand, I use my left hand to lovingly flick off the crowd as the opening synths from the track play. I'm alive.

An adventure was getting ready to start, and luckily this was the last stop on the tour, so I was finishing it up just in time to start it. I turn to Lemon and the rest of the band.

"We're opening with Falling Star," I tell them. "Then we're gonna go right into Cast A Spell. Cool?"

They looked a bit confused at first. Falling Star wasn't exactly a song to open with, but I wanted to go ahead and get it out of the way. Ironically enough, I wrote the song as a message to any girl who I felt completely and utterly drawn to. Didn't happen often honestly. So I knew she'd get it.

Lemon shrugged and dropped the beat, banging out a computerized drumroll on the pads of the electronic snares. With childlike excitement in my voice, I look into the crowd to find Luna exactly where I knew she'd be. As we made eye contact, I walked to the edge of the stage, took a deep breath, and prepared my voice to hit a falsetto in the key of G. To no one but Luna, I sang the lyrics to one of my favorite songs that I've ever written.

I swore I saw you fall to Earth

Did you fall to Earth, did you fall to Earth

I swore I saw you fall to Earth

Did you fall to Earth, did you fall to Earth

Calm down baby don't stress

We can make a love spell worthy of rest

Calm down baby don't stress

We can make a love spell worthy of rest

Her aura is shining, shining

Full on that shit is shining, shining

I know mine is damn near blinding, blinding

Her aura is shining, shining

As the music for this tune came to an end, and I hummed out the last note, the chords for Cast A Spell began to play. I looked to Luna, who was biting her lip at me, I smiled proudly. To my everlasting pleasure, a mosh pit began to open up in the middle of the crowd.

CHAPTER SIX

CARRYING
TORCHES

"Look, I know for sure that I said no goddamn onions in this shrimp fried rice," said an upset Mecca Saunders, who was pointing at his freshly cooked, but now unwanted, Chinese style carryout meal. He had been waiting for thirty minutes in Good Taste, a Chinese restaurant on the VCU campus that wasn't too far from his dorm. But now, he was officially running late for band rehearsal.

"We can fix that though," the pink haired girl behind the counter said to him with a Jersey accent as strong as his own New York one. "I don't see why you trippin' so hard over this."

"Because now I gotta wait another fifteen to thirty minutes for my food," said Mecca as he scratched his beard in annoyance. "Baby, I got shit to do."

"We all got shit to do," she told him. "Do I look like I actually want to be cooking rice and egg rolls all damn day?"

"Really?" Mecca asked as he stared into the black pupils of those beautifully narrow eyes of hers. "You really gonna ask me that? That's too easy baby. I'm hungry as hell, I'm just gonna take the damn rice."

"That's ya best bet, because you working on my last nerve," the girl told him as she folded her arms. She pursed her lips and rolled her neck at him, which caused the young obnoxious man to laugh. Mecca gave her the money in exchange for the bag of food he'd just handed back to her. As he left out, he heard the girl scream, "I hope you get a lame ass fortune cookie too!"

"Yeah, yeah," Mecca stopped at the door, turned around to her and said, "Yo, you're lucky you're cute. Because really, I should leave a bad Yelp review."

"Oh yeah?" She asked, trying not to laugh at his antics in that moment.

"Goddamn right. And it would be just about you, and your rudeness." As he pointed his finger at her, he finished with, "Thank you though."

"I love your locs!" he heard her scream as he left out. The compliment made him smile, encouraging him take his hair out of its bun and let his locs swing. He smiled and stroked his beard a few times as he thought about where he'd eat his meal. Then it dawned on him, outside. Why not enjoy the day right?

He walked two blocks down Grace Street, taking a seat on his favorite green bench right in front of Strange Matter, the venue he'd be playing at with his friends later on that week. Instead of going over the bass parts for his band's songs in his mind, like he should have been doing, he put his headphones on and pressed play on his Cosmic S12. "In Bloom" by Nirvana, his favorite band ever, began to play.

As he took his food out of the bag, he noticed that a tall, young, short-haired brown-toned man was sitting in the car parked in front of him, an orange 2002 Chevy Impala that'd obviously been broken into. The man, who looked to be between 25 & 30, thin but toned in frame, was in pretty busted up shape. Mecca began to stand up but the man had already spotted him and stretched his right arm out, motioning him to stay put. Sporting a large gash on his forehead, a bloody nose, and what looked to be a broken arm from what Mecca had just seen, the man seemed determined to take care of himself.

Ignoring the warning, Mecca stood up to approach the car and ask the man if he needed some obvious help. Out of nowhere, three men popped up from underneath the ground, all of them wearing black trench coats smothered in mud. Each of the man's attackers wore masks made of stone with small holes at the nostrils for ventilation and black glass for their vision. Their arms were also covered in stone, wrapped around their limbs as obvious armor doubling as weapons. Mecca's eyes went wide. He stopped breathing for a moment. The disbelief was too real for his body. Mecca had just eye-witnessed real life Earthers come from under the ground. For the first time in a very long time, he found himself mentally frozen, debating in his head on what he should do next.

The men inched closer to the car, totally ignoring Mecca's presence as well as that of any other bystander. The injured man inside of the vehicle looked at them with a very nonchalant expression across his face. He must have changed his mind about running away, because he got out of the car and let the men surrounding him move in even closer to him. The mysterious and battered man continued to hold his arm in place, which was definitely broken and very possibly bent out of shape. There was even blood seeping through various tears in his teal long-sleeve PILA shirt. He began smiling at them proudly, his bloody teeth still intact.

Mecca knew from looking at the man that he was in no condition to fight all of these people. His hero complex kicked in, and soon Mecca was quietly backing away from them all, only to throw his cup of sweet tea at one of the Earthers' heads, his food at another one, and then he started charging at that one with full force. The

Earther that was hit with the ice cold beverage turned his head around slowly, or cockily, only to catch a left hook to the jaw from the brave, golden glove trained onlooker. The bruised up individual who'd just received random assistance took full advantage of the distraction and, much to Mecca's dual surprise/excitement, shot beams of intensified light straight through the heads of the other two Earthers from the palm of his left hand. His good arm. Both ops died right there. Then the stranger used his palm to shoot a beam of light at the Earther that Mecca had punched in the face.

Mecca didn't know why he hadn't pieced it together before, but the man was a Lighter.

"Dude, are you okay?" he asked the mysterious Universian.

"Yeah," the Lighter said with a glare, "I'm just wounded real fuckin' bad and bleeding to death internally. That's all."

"Sorry, dumb question," Mecca nervously admitted. "We gotta get you to a hospital."

Mecca walked the man over to the bench he'd been originally sitting on when this all happened.

The man shook his head and said, "I should be asking why you decided to help me."

"I don't know, it was the right thing to do."

"So you just go around helping random people in need?" the man chuckled a bit. "You like a Black Robin Hood or somethin', kid?"

"Nah, I just…"

"Well it's nice to meet you, Black Robin Hood, my name's Tevin," he told him. "Tevin Torch. Currently, the general for the Universian Light Army in North America. But that seems to be changing as of right now. Shit…"

Tevin winced in pain. After taking a deep breath he locked eyes with Mecca again and said, "Okay. And you are?"

"I'm Malcolm Saunders. But all of my friends call me Mecca. So, there's really a war between the Universian races then?"

"I'm not going to answer that…but yes." Tevin laughed a little but quickly began cringing in pain, coughing up blood onto his shirt next. "Get out of here kid. Cops'll probably be here soon. And trust me, you don't wanna be here for that."

"Uhh, you sure?" Mecca asked him with a bit of worry. Tevin didn't say anything. He just gave him a look, and the look said: "leave." So Mecca grabbed his food and power walked the hell away from that crime scene. He didn't even think about turning around. He was hightailing it to Omar's house as fast as his feet would take him. Mecca had seen enough BS in his twenty years to know that a dark person, human, elf, or whatever, was not safe near dead bodies.

When Mecca finally got to Omar's house, who was the drummer for his band, Crescent Sun, he found his bandmates already in full swing of rehearsal. He looked at Keith, his best friend of eleven years, as well as the guitarist and lead vocalist for Crescent Sun. As soon as he saw Mecca, Keith pulled down his black, silk face off, revealing the two Eartian fangs that always rest outside of any Eartian's mouth. This definitely meant that he was pissed. Omar didn't look too pleased by the display of tardiness either. Placing an empty Chinese food box on the table, Mecca's brain scrambled for the right words to say before getting chewed out.

After thirty seconds of repeating the word "um," Mecca finally spoke English and said, "Something happened."

"Obviously, bruh," Keith said. "I know this is only your second time being late, so we're not that pissed. But it's been an hour and a half. So we're still pretty pissed."

"Yeah man," Omar chimed in, "if Crescent Sun is going to be the next Nirvana, we gotta do everything right. That means no showing up to practice an hour and a half late."

"Okay, bad example," Mecca said as his nose scrunched up in confusion, "That's exactly the kind of shit that Kurt used to do when he was alive. You know what his band became? Nirvana."

"Yeah," Omar replied, "and now that nigga dead. So we gotta do everything right."

"He's got a point, Mecca," Keith piggybacked. "What's the point of us forming our class schedules around rehearsal times if you're gonna be late. I know y'all loved those Nirvana freaks and all, but I'm aiming to kick their ass for real."

"Look, my bad," Mecca said while walking to pick up his bass guitar. "Keith, I'll talk to you about this after rehearsal."

"Sure," Keith said. "Let's just wrap up with this so we can catch Sammy's skate competition." The bandmates shrugged and began to play a song that they had entitled "Thin Rivers." After rehearsal was over, Mecca and Keith caught a Duber together to catch the VCU skate competition. Their other childhood friend, Sammy, was a participant this year and a sure bet as a projected winner. On the way there, Mecca decided it'd be best to tell Keith about what actually happened to him earlier that day. Not sure why he picked the Duber ride to tell him, but that's what happened.

"You're not gonna believe what happened to me today bro," Mecca began.

"Try your luck then," Keith said through his sharp fang smile. He never wore his face mask during rehearsal.

"So I'm leaving Good Taste, right," Mecca began, "and I'm already a little behind schedule because I had that African studies essay to finish up, right. And I see this Mexican-lookin' dude sitting in his car and he looks beat the fuck up, yo. I mean, beat the fuck up. Then, out of nowhere, like three or four dudes in dirty ass trench coats pop up outta the ground. So, I throw a cup at one of they heads, right. Homie tried to turn around all tough so I ran up and POP! Knocked his ass clean the fuck out, right. And then, the Mexican dude from the car used his hand like it was a gun and shot a beam of light at all of 'em. And he killed them Earthers, man. They dead. And by now, I think he dead too."

"Bullshiiiittt!!" Keith replied quickly.

"I'm serious man. The dude's name was Tevin Torch. He said he was…"

"Wait, wait, wait…," Keith said quickly, cutting him off. "Hold up, bruh. Tevin Torch is the leader of the American Lighters."

"Yep, that's him. Dude, you're such a dork for knowing that."

"Nattie!" Keith exclaimed. "Is this some kind of joke?! You really expect my black ass to believe you?"

"Yeah," Mecca told him in almost defensive tone. "Why would I lie to you about this shit? Sammy wouldn't believe me or care. But I didn't actually think this shit was really real until today."

"The Universian War is serious, Mecca. You need to be more aware of what's going on around you, man."

"Yo," Mecca exclaimed while cutting his eyes at his friend, "tell me how I can focus on a race of people that don't want to be found. They DO. NOT. WANT. TO BE FOUND. You know how many times when we were growing up people would tell me they saw a frickin' Universian and then their IG post of the footage would get deleted… or their whole account would get deleted?! No media coverage on their asses! No nothing! How can I be aware of that, Keith? Please tell me."

Keith looked out the window for a second before answering his patiently waiting good homie. Keith was the friend Mecca knew he could tell this stuff to without being judged for it. Average in height at 5'8 but built like a linebacker thanks to his Eartian DNA, Keith Dammet always felt like both a grown man and a child all at once. Maybe that was because of his strong wisdom yet his vulgar sense of humor, or maybe it was just because he was bald at the age of twenty. But aside from being a good singer, and a great guitarist, he was very much into the conspiracy theory of the Universian people. He held memberships on a number of different forums and chat rooms, and even had a few contraband books on the hypernatural race. All things to expect from a Gen Z anthropogeny major on full ride at VCU.

But with no witty comeback, Keith said abruptly, "Look, bruh, I told yo' ass they were really out here fucking shit up. Did I not? Don't take it out on me that you're still in shock from seeing three people get laser beamed to death, with yo' sweet-tea throwing ass. Listen to ya boy, bruh!"

After an awkward silence, Mecca said, "It was fried rice."

After another awkward silence, Keith said, "Cool ass day for you though right?"

Mecca then responded in an obnoxiously high pitched voice, "Cool as a motherfuckeeer."

The quiet Duber driver, a light-brown skinned girl with big poofy pigtails named Shelby, dropped them off at the skate park and tonight, the place was packed with all sorts of people. She had been really quiet the whole ride. They took a seat on some bleachers and looked for Sammy. They spotted him standing next to a rail holding his skateboard listening to music. His headphones were over his baseball cap, as they always were, and he looked utterly engulfed in his own zone. The main thing that Mecca noticed was that everyone in the competition was warming up a bit, except for Sammy Hedges.

Sammy was the other childhood friend of Mecca and Keith. A skinny, fair-toned, 19-year-old kid with family roots in Cuba, a swimmer's build and a mind of gold, Sammy found his peace doing wild tricks on skateboards. He was the quietest out of the three of them, as his parents always had him studying or had him locked inside to do what they deemed as suitable extracurricular activities for their child. And in their eleven/twelve year span of being friends (Mecca and his family moved into the Harlem neighborhood they were raised in a year after his friends did), he'd actually only met Sammy's folks twice. There were even a few times he'd knock on Mecca's door dirty as hell with tears in his eyes asking for a place to stay, claiming weird punishments for getting B's and C's. Without question, Mecca would always let him in.

"NOW," the DJ began on his microphone, "THE MOMENT YOU'VE ALL BEEN WAITING FOR!!! TIME TO KICK THIS SHIT OFF!!! THE FIRST ANNUAL 2019 VCU SKATE LIFE COMPETITION!!!" The crowd went absolutely nuts upon hearing this. The DJ began mixing between a few records in order to get the crowd even more excited, but once they began to play Dizzy Blu's "Stacks Up," the excitement on Sammy's face showed that he was officially ready. Sammy looked over at Mecca and Keith, still wearing that smile filled with excitement, and held his board in the air. This was always his symbol to let them know that he was about to take it all the way.

All of the contestants were named and the competition began. The first event was a freestyle challenge. Sammy scored a 98, putting him at first place, and proceeded into the next round where he scored a 95, which bumped him to second. By the time the final round came, Sammy had pulled out an array of versatile tricks that seemed magically surreal, leaving the judges completely stunned. He finished off his run by performing a triple kick-flip from the halfpipe and landing with his feet on his board, behind the top of the halfpipe. The crowd went absolutely nuts.

"IF SAMMY DOESN'T WIN," the DJ screamed into the microphone, "I AM NEVER DOING A SKATING EVENT HERE AGAIN! THAT SHIT WAS SICK!! WHAT ARE YOU?!" The competition was now over, and all of the contestants waited to hear the outcome, although, everyone knew who the winner would unanimously be.

"AND THE WINNER OF THIS YEAR'S SKATE OFF IS….SAMMY HEDGES!!!"

The crowd went crazy with applause. Keith and Mecca both ran over to their friend to congratulate him on his big win. It was such a euphoric feeling for Sammy that his naturally calm composure was noticeably being challenged by all of the cheers for his performance. The other contestants came over to congratulate him as well, but were passed by a large amount of eager kids asking Sammy to sign their boards. Amongst all of the chaos, someone managed to get through the clutter of people to personally grab Sammy's attention. A young brown-skinned man dressed in a vintage 86er's throwback jersey and Balmain jeans tapped the young champion skater on the shoulder.

"Great show bruh," he said handing him his card. Sammy took it, but he couldn't speak. This was the first time he'd been starstruck. He was looking at Rollo Brandon, the 24 year old skateboarding phenomenon that the world was calling the greatest since Anthony Hawk.

"Thanks," was all Sammy could get out before Rollo patted him on the back and walked off.

"We'll talk soon," Rollo shouted without looking back. Yeah, he really was cool like that. Keith and Mecca started yelling and shaking Sammy's shoulders out of excitement. They were more than happy to lose their shit on their friend's behalf. The young Cuban-born college skateboard champion just stood there smiling, taking it all in. He then turned to his right, looking at Mecca with a smile.

"My dawg," he said with a sigh full of nothing but satisfaction, "bruh, I'm hungry."

It almost goes without saying that Sammy was stopped by every single skate-team owner in attendance on their way out of that place. Phone numbers, email, social media, they gave him all of it. Just that quickly, Sammy Hedges had become another rockstar on VCU's campus, joining his two best friends in the world of viral popularity. After they left the competition, the three young buzzing stars decided that Bodillaz, a quesadilla joint on Broad St., would be the best place to celebrate Sammy's big win. On weekends, Bodillaz is never not poppin'.

"Dude," Keith began, keeping dramatic slowness in his words, "that was awesome."

"Thanks, man," Sammy said munching on his fries. "I honestly thought I was gonna fall on that last trick."

"Dude you never fall," Mecca told him. "The day you fall from skating is gonna be the day I pop a guitar string."

"Another good show from our token skater," Keith said laughing. "What would we do without you, Sammy? Other than not attend skate competitions."

"Excuse me," came a light, feminine voice from behind them. They turned around to see a very, very pretty young lady walking up from the booth behind them. Her other two friends, both equally as gorgeous, one was a Nigerian girl with an afro and the other was an Arabic girl with light brown eyes sporting a purple face mask. They were looking back and giggling as they observed what would happen.

"Hi," Sammy said while smiling at her shyly, something that he does naturally but is completely aware of.

"You're Sammy Hedges, right?"

"Yep," he said taking a bite from his quesadilla. "You are?"

"I'm Crystal," she took a fry from him and nibbled on it. "I have a biology class with you. I honestly had no idea you could skate like that."

"Are you a freshman?" Keith asked her. "Because last year Sammy was tearing VCU up in the streets. Everybody here knows what he does."

"Well I'm actually a transfer student from ODU, I'm a sophomore," she said. She then paused and looked at Keith and Mecca, tilting her head before saying, "I know you guys from somewhere. Do you two play in a band?"

"Crescent Sun," Mecca stated.

"Told you!" One of the girl's friends screamed from behind the dining booth.

"Word!" Crystal exclaimed. "I saw you guys open up for The Avenue last year when we went to NYU's homecoming. You dudes were awesome."

"Thanks," Mecca said, now letting down his locs from its bun. "Yeah that was a fun show. We're playing in New York again soon too. Y'all show come with us when we go."

"That'd be cool," said one of the girls who hadn't given their name yet. She giggled and turned away from Mecca's glance shyly.

"So we have the best skater on campus and two members from Crescent Sun all in a Burger King talking to you right now," Keith said with a grin, "just a bunch of future, world renowned rockstars right here. It's three of us, then there's you as well as two of your friends...we should all totally catch a move right now."

Crystal laughed and said, "Well, I have a few bottles back in my room if you guys wanna come and drink with us."

"Let's go," Mecca said as he and his friends stood up to leave with their new companions. This day was just getting better and better for him.

The trio definitely ended up in Crystal's dorm with her other two friends, and they all had a few drinks. Then a few turned into quite a few, and they all ended up getting drunk. Then dancing around a bit which, luckily, led to the smoking of some sweet ganja. After a few make-out sessions with the girls, Keith ended up in Crystal's bedroom. The blue-eyed, dark-browns Eartian singer charms worked in his favor again. Sammy and Mecca exchanged numbers with their new friends and then they went back to their own respective places of rest, their dorm rooms. When Mecca got back to his room, he cut on the light and saw Tevin sitting in his chair.

"What the fuck?!" Mecca yelled backing up. "Yo I'm calling the cops!"

"Call the cops, and I'll glow so bright your eyeballs will melt outta ya fucking skull," Tevin said sternly as he stood up. Mecca put his phone back in his pocket after hearing that. "Sit down. I need to talk to you."

"How the hell did you find me, man?" Mecca sat down on his bed. "And how long you been in my room?"

"Don't worry about any of that right now," Tevin told him. He sat back in the chair and grabbed his stomach.

"Did you get your side patched up?"

"Yeah, but it's not doing much. The Earthers that attacked me, one of them was able to get some sharp as shit tiny rocks stuck in my stomach. My brother can't stop the bleeding this time. I'm dying, Mecca."

"Damn," Mecca said in shock. "Well, don't die here,. I don't want people thinking that I'm the one that killed you."

Tevin cracked a smile and then let out the words that would change Malcolm Saunders forever, "I want you to have my light."

"What?"

"I want to give you my light, kid. You deserve it."

"But I…"

Tevin's finger lit up like E.T.'s. And before Mecca knew it, the Mexican Lighter's glowing finger was gently resting was on Mecca's forehead. The young bassist felt the transfer of power in his eyes first. They felt as if they were literally on fire. Everything had become a blur of blinding light. He wanted to scream, but couldn't for some reason. Then a strong surge of energy came over his body. He looked at his hands and arms, all glowing like a fluorescent light bulb; he could even see his veins, which looked like an electric current flowing through him. The light show emitting from his body began to die down and Mecca dropped onto one knee panting heavily, feeling as if he had just been stuck underwater for hours. He looked up and saw Tevin disappearing, but slowly.

He was turning into little tiny specks of light, as if he was actually composed of a community of fireflies.

"Take care kid," Tevin said as he vanished. "Everything you want to know will be answered soon…and punch my brother when you get the chance."

Tevin was gone. Mecca couldn't breathe, let alone hold himself up. He felt tired and heavy. With all of the strength he had left in his aching, hot-to-the-touch body, he dragged himself onto his bed. And as soon as he hit the pillow, he slept.

****

Mecca woke up rubbing his eyes. He felt heavy, as if his body weighed much more than it usually did. He lifted his arms and dropped them. Definitely heavier than usual. Rubbing his eyes some more, he stood up but was greeted with strange chills that coursed throughout his entire body starting at his feet. Still dressed in the clothes from the previous day, he sat back down and tried to think about the last thing that happened to him. Did he fall? Did he get jumped? His mind flashed to an image of Tevin Torch turning into fireflies.

"He died," Mecca said to himself. There was a sudden loud knock at his door. He got up, practically forcing his legs to walk. Looking through the peephole on his door, he saw Keith and Sammy standing there with Mr. Young, the oversized brown man with gray hair riddled dorm director. He opened it and they all just kind of stared at him.

"What?" Mecca blurted out.

"Bruh, we've called you like a million times," Keith told him through his black "Distinguished Crooks" branded face mask. "Check your phone."

Mecca then pulled his phone out of his pocket to see 52 missed calls and 73 unread text messages from an array of people, but mostly from Keith, Omar, and Sammy.

Mr. Young then added, "Your friends have been worried sick about you."

There was a long pause.

"Why?" Mecca blurted out again.

"Man it's like eight o'clock," Sammy told him.

"We went to sleep at four in the morning, bro," Mecca said. "So I've only been sleep for four hours. Why the hell are y'all so mad about that? It's Saturday, ain't it? We ain't got rehearsals or class or nothin' today."

"It's eight o'clock at night, dumbass," Keith said.

"Watch your mouth, Dammet," Mr. Young said.

"You can't tell me to watch my mouth, only to curse at me yourself, sir," Keith said slickly.

"That's your last name," Mr. Young said, irritably.

"Then put a mister in front of it," Keith told him. "But we're here to focus on Mecca, Mr. Young. So, Mecca, are you okay?"

"Yeah," Mecca said, fighting back a laugh. "Tired. Might be catching a cold or something, but I'm okay."

"Well if you're okay, I'm going back downstairs to finish my honey bun," Mr. Young said walking off.

"Fat fucker," Sammy said under his breath.

"I been asleep for fifteen hours?" Mecca asked aloud.

"Yeah," Keith said. "We've been worried like hell."

"Oh shit," Sammy said, with a weird look of concern. "It really has been fifteen hours."

"That's close to a coma," Mecca said. "Damn, well…" Mecca's neighbor Penny came out of her room and looked at Mecca with an evil face.

"Hey jackass," she started, "next time you wanna have a light show at four in the morning, how about you warn people first. Better yet, just don't do it."

"Yo, fuck you, Penny," Mecca shouted. "That's why don't nobody like yo' ass now."

"I don't care," she said. "I know a few nights ago Keith loved this ass."

"Hey," Keith said pointing at her. "Shut up." Penny blew him a kiss and walked away laughing.

"Light show?" Sammy asked aloud.

"Yeah," Keith wondered as well. "What the hell does she mean?"

"Guys, I'll meet ya'll in the cafeteria for dinner," Sammy told them. "I've gotta get something." With that, Sammy sped off.

"Alright man," Keith said pushing past Mecca and walking into the room. "The Universians have this book that they call the Book of The Ages, kinda like their bible. It states that if a Lighter transfers his light to a regular Human, the Human must rest for at least thirteen hours. You slept for fifteen after a 'light show' went off."

"Glad to have you as a friend," Mecca said sitting on his bed. "You just figured out the whole story."

"Holy shit," Keith smiled uncontrollably. "Holy shit! Dude you weren't lying. You're a Lighter! You've gotta tell Sammy."

"Wait," Mecca said confused. "You aren't concerned?"

"Concerned?" Keith chuckled. "Nattie boy, hell yeah! Do you have any idea what's about to happen to you?"

"No," Mecca said, "but I'm sure you're about to tell me."

"Pretty much, you're gonna get engulfed in a whole different world. From what I've read, there's been battles all across the world between Lighters and Earthers ever since the war started in 2004.

"Thing is, if someone sees it or reports the battles to like a newspaper or a news team or some shit, they get tracked down and sworn to secrecy. The world you're about to be a part of, I wouldn't wish it on my least favorite Wiccan, no cap."

"So this whole war is basically some secret conspiracy shit?"

"Pretty much," Keith said as he put his dreads into a ponytail. "But I'll help you out as much as possible. They'll probably find you sometime tomorrow."

"Who?" Mecca asked concerned.

"The other Lighters. You're gonna have to be a part of the war. You have Tevin Torch's light. They're gonna need you. Good thing you got good in combat courses growing up. Because...damn."

With that statement, and a shake of his head, Keith dapped his friend up and departed. Mecca got in the shower and got dressed. He and Keith met back up with Sammy to go to dinner. Then they went back to Keith's off-campus house to chill for a bit. While in there, Mecca picked up Keith's black book on Universians.

"If there aren't any legal publications on the war then how the hell you get this book?" Mecca asked.

"It's an underground thing," Keith explained as he took his face mask off. "Copies are made in secrecy and certain bookstores sell them under the table. Mainly comic book stores."

"I don't see why you guys are into that stuff," Sammy said. "If there's some shit going on with them, we shouldn't be involved. Doesn't seem safe."

"This is real shit here, Sammy," Keith said while plucking a few notes on his guitar. "These people might blow the world up. Hopefully they take the Wiccans first. I hate all the Wiccans."

"When you guys blow up," Sammy said to Mecca, "make sure he doesn't talk in interviews. Everybody's gonna figure out quick that Keith Dammet of Crescent Sun is a total frickin' racist. Weren't you just bumping Warlock the other day?"

"I don't know," Mecca blurted out. "What if he's right to be keeping up with this stuff, man?"

"Dude," Sammy said laughing. "You're not seriously…" Sammy was cut off by his beeper going off. "Gotta go." Then he quickly grabbed his skateboard and jetted out of the door.

"I'm gonna go ahead and bounce too," Mecca said as he pounded fists with Keith.

"Yo, Mecca," Keith called to him. "Be safe going back to your room, bruh."

"I'll be good," Mecca told his boy. Then he headed out.

Mecca put on his headphones and started listening to Beck. He noticed that every time he walked passed a street light, it would flicker a bit. He wondered if it was because of his supposed new power, which he was too afraid to try to use, or if he was just crazy. He paused his music and stopped to stand in front of one of the street lights, looking up at it. He focused on it with the intent of making the light bulb explode. It flickered and flickered until it finally exploded, shattering the glass inside of it. His jaw dropped. Had that really just happened? Was someone around to see? That's when he sniffed the air, catching a strong whiff of what he knew to be blueberry yum-yum.

"You know you can absorb them, right?" he heard a kind voice say.

Mecca turned around quickly to see the beautiful face of a light-brown skinned girl standing under a street light smoking a backwood blunt. A mischievous smile sat on her face. Getting a closer look at her, he could tell that she was mixed. He was right to guess African with Indian heritage, and she appeared to be Human. Maybe. He quickly realized it was Shelby, the girl who had just given them a Duber ride the day before. On this day, her hair was pulled back into two puffy ponytails. Around her neck was a copper necklace with a clear quartz crystal charm wrapped in wire.

"Uhh," Mecca uttered as he looked around. He nervously took off his headphones and said, "What?"

"I said you can absorb them," she said again, putting one hand in the air. "The lights of course. They pretty much belong to us."

The light inside of the streetlight above her shot directly into her hand, and she was literally holding it like a ball. Mecca looked at it and felt as if he was staring into a magical orb. She handed him the light and to his surprise, he was able to hold it.

"So," the girl said circling him, "Tevin actually decided to jump you his light, huh?"

"Well, it definitely would seem that way," Mecca said, trying to follow her movements. "Yeah, I guess so."

"You got a name?"

"Malcolm. But everybody calls me Mecca though."

"Mecca?" the girl stopped walking for a second and then continued.

She stopped quickly and put a glowing finger in his face. "Well hello, Mecca. Nice to see you again. My name is Shelby Knox. I'm here to bring you back to Corona City with me."

"Uhh, nah," Mecca said with his eyes glued to her glowing finger. "I'm, uhh, I'm definitely not gonna do that. I have a test tomorrow. And band rehearsals…and we're opening up for Warlock The MC next week."

"Warlock The MC, huh? I love Warlock! That's pretty cool."

"Can you put your finger down now?"

"Nope," she said. Shelby then pushed it a bit closer. "You're coming back with me. It's either I knock you out, or you just come willingly."

Mecca stared at her finger and noticed that the glow was starting to spread to the rest of her hand. He figured that she was gathering more energy for a stronger blast if he refused, and after sleeping for fifteen hours he didn't really want to get put into another pseudo coma. So he just nodded.

"Glad you see things my way," Shelby said, as she finally put down her glowing hand. "Don't worry, you're not gonna have to stay there forever. Only when we need you. But, that might be pretty often. C'mon, Mecca."

The girl started walking off and Mecca just kind of looked at her in wonder. He wasn't exactly sure if following her was a good idea. This Shelby girl seemed a tad bit...off.

"Hey! Come on!" she yelled at him.

Mecca followed her lead. They ended up walking to an abandoned dorm on his campus where it was rumored that someone had been murdered.

"Nobody ever comes here," Mecca stated.

"That's the point, mister obvious," she said with a laugh. "Check this out." She held her hand out, and a ball of light appeared with blue electricity sparking from it. The force of the orb she held released a powerful gust of wind, causing both of their hair to start swirling around a bit. The crystal charm on her neck began to glow at the same pulse as the orb in her hands, steady and slow. Your boy Mecca couldn't do anything but stare at it.

"Wow," Mecca said with a stunned face, "that shit looks awesome."

"It is awesome!!" Shelby exclaimed with excitement. "Touch it. It'll make you really, really strong."

Mecca looked at the girl, who was wearing a wide grin from ear to ear and thought about her words. He still hadn't used his new powers yet, so he wondered if he touched this sphere, would he start off stronger than what he already was. He shrugged and placed his hands upon the light. All of a sudden he felt a big surge...of nothing.

"I don't feel anything," he told her.

"I know," Shelby said with that wide grin of hers. Then she shouted, "HOME!!"

Mecca felt himself slip into the ball itself. He couldn't do anything to stop it, but even if he could, he wouldn't have. The feeling that the light gave him when it took over his body was sensational. It was as if he was invincible for the moment.

He looked around and saw that he was flying through what looked like a tube of some sort. It was black with white swirls coating it all over. It looked like they were floating into a rift in outer space. He looked forward and saw that they were nearing a light. Looking to his left, Mecca saw Shelby. She looked gray. Her smile was gone until she noticed Mecca looking at her. She grinned right back, letting him know not to worry.

When the light got so bright that he couldn't see, Mecca decided to stare harder. All he saw was white. Then he hit the ground landing face first. Shelby was standing over him laughing giddily.

"You looked into the light, didn't you?" she asked, still chuckling at him.

"Yeah, I did," he told her.

"The sun shines brighter here," she said with a smile. "We make sure of that."

Mecca's eyes were having trouble adjusting to the abnormally bright place he was in. It looked like he was in a mechanical wonderland with skyscrapers everywhere. The sky was bluer than any hue of it he'd seen before, and the sun in the middle of the sky shone brighter than he could've imagined. The second sun in the sky, however, seemed to be orbiting around the one in the center. Yep, a city with two suns. It was angled at a perfect ninety-degree angle. The air felt much cleaner than anywhere he'd ever visited before too.

People were moving about all sorts of ways, and all of the cars there seemed to run off of solar energy. He paused a moment in disbelief, just taking it all in.

"This is Corona City," Shelby explained. "Most beautiful fucking place in the entire world."

"I'm not gonna argue with that," he said, his face still in awe.

"Well, come with me, there's a few people you need to meet."

Mecca followed the strange girl into a big metallic building with a huge tinted window at the top left to it. It had a round roof and it reminded Mecca of something that could've been made in ancient Greece if they had the technology back then.

The halls were white with marble floors. On the walls were pictures of people doing amazing things. Some were fighting, some were building shit, and Tevin was in almost every picture. Mecca started realizing that with Tevin's light inside of him, he had huge shoes to fill. But he wasn't trying to do that at all.

They approached an opened door leading to a high-tech laboratory with an open roof exactly twelve feet in the air. Hanging from middle of the top of the opening, was a chandelier type of object made out of solar panels. Shelby pointed to a thin but toned framed, long-haired man sitting at a computer. He wore rectangular reading glasses and an orange baseball cap backwards on his head. Mecca immediately thought that this dude looked like a nerdier version of Tevin.

"That's Tevin's brother, Tony," she told him. Tony heard his name and looked up at Shelby, catching her gaze.

"Tony!" Shelby shouted excitedly. She then rushed over to hug him. "I found him. This is the guy with your brother's light. Meet Mecca Saunders."

"Hey, Shelby," Tony said in a raspy baritone voice, hugging her back. He went over to look at the newcomer in his lab. "You're Mecca, huh?" Tony said looking at him. "Tevin said that you seemed like a very nice guy."

"I get that a lot," Mecca said.

"Good," Tony said as he adjusted his glasses. "Have you used your powers yet?"

"No sir, I haven't."

"Also good," Tony didn't look up from his computer as he spoke. "You're going straight to Dominic for training."

"Hell no," came a voice from behind them. Mecca turned around to see a fairly tall, slender built fair-skinned woman with short black hair and a cigarette in her mouth. Her attitude and swagger gave him straight Colombiana vibes. I mean, she looked really, tough. You ever just see someone who looks like they've been through a lot and ain't afraid to go through more? That's how this chick looked. She wore a pink spaghetti strap top with cut-off jean shorts. Her arms and face were a bit dirty too, but Mecca wasn't sure if she'd just finished fighting someone or building something. And honestly, he was afraid to ask.

"Hey, Rita," Shelby said as the lady approached.

"I wanna train this kid, Tony," Rita explained.

"You don't train anyone, remember?" Tony told her.

"Who said that ridiculous shit?" she asked sternly.

"You did," Tony said staring at her.

"I'm training him, Tony," Rita said. "If this kid is really carrying Tevin's light, then he's going to need some serious control. No disrespect to the old man, but you know Dominic just can't give him that kind of focus at the moment."

"Fine," Tony said as he sat back down behind his laptop. "Start learning, Mecca."

Rita puffed out a perfect smoke ring that hit Mecca square in his face as she gave him a super stern look. Shelby just grinned without saying anything. She motioned for them to follow.

"Shelby," Rita started, "I want you to come with us. Tell me if I'm being a good teacher or not."

"I can't," Shelby said. "Seven and I are supposed to be finding out which Earther killed Tevin."

"That's supposed to be my job," Rita said in a somewhat snappy tone.

"Hey, you take that up with Tony," Shelby snapped back. "And put out ya damn cigarette."

Rita puffed a ring in her face, making Shelby's face turn a bit. Then Shelby hugged her and departed. When Mecca and Rita were finished walking they were in front of a square metal building.

"Well, let's start your training, Mecca," Rita said throwing down her cigarette. They walked into the building and Mecca noticed all of the training equipment instantly, it was a gym. The ring in the middle made him feel like he did when he first took up boxing lessons at age seven. He put down his book bag and walked up to a punching bag.

"So did you and Tevin have a thing?" he asked Rita as he took a swing at the punching bag.

She walked over to where he was standing and took a few swings at him. He dodged the barrage of attacks, barely, and fell on his bottom. She began throwing light blasts at him, busting a few of the punching bags in there. He ran behind a tall pole trying to hide.

"C'mon Mecca," Rita said in a sweet voice. "Where's that shrimp fried rice punch power you had when you met Tevin?"

"How'd you know about that?"

"We spoke to him before he died. How do you think we found you? Hell, how do you think he found you?"

Mecca thought back to that room full of computers, and it finally hit him, Tony was some kind of hacker genius. But he quickly realized that this was the wrong time to be thinking about this because he took a shot to the jaw from Rita.

"Damn," Mecca said grabbing his jaw and backing away from her. "That really hurt."

"Catch," was the only response that Rita gave. She sent a speeding ball of light charging towards him. He caught it, but it was still pressing towards him. The pressure caused him to buckle a bit and drop to one knee.

Mecca ended up sending the energy ball flying back at Rita. She dodged it and was surprised to see that Mecca had his own light blast ready to shoot. For a second, Rita thought she was looking at Tevin. Then the blast shot, and she waved it off as if it was nothing.

"Not bad," Rita said, taking out a cigarette.

"Not bad?" Mecca said panting. He was sweating massively. "You treated that shit like it was nothing."

"It wasn't," Rita told him. "Just because you make a big construction, doesn't mean it's gonna be that strong."

"That doesn't even make sense," he said while sitting down. Rita went into the kitchen to grab him a bottle of water out of the refrigerator.

"If a light bulb is big, that doesn't automatically mean it's bright," she said handing him the water. "It's all in how much power is put into it. The Lighters are like light bulbs, little baby."

"So our powers are measured in watts?"

"Exactly, that's literally how we measure our powers."

"Nice," he said feeling accomplished for that guess.

"Well," Rita said, pulling him to his feet, "you've got a lot to learn, but you need to head back to school now. We'll come to get you on Thursday and pick back up with your training."

"Ok cool." Then he remembered. "Wait, I can't. I have rehearsal Thursday for our show on Friday. We're opening for Warlock The MC."

"Oh really? That'd be great news if I actually gave a fuck. Thursday, no excuses. And if you give Shelby a hard time, I'm kicking your ass like you're an Earther. Got it?"

"Damn…hell yeah, I got it."

****

Later on that night, Mecca found himself sitting in his room making a light construct in the shape of a triangle. He figured if he could teach himself a little bit that it might get Rita off of his back. He was making the light all through his body and having a good amount of fun with it too when someone knocked on his door. Mecca looked through the peephole to see it was Sammy at the door.

"Yo," Mecca said as he opened the door.

"What's up," Sammy said walking in. Mecca noticed something was a bit off.

"You all good?" he asked him.

"I should be asking you that," Sammy said sitting on the bed. "Me and Keith heard you went walking off with some weird-looking hot chick last night. What's up with that?"

"Ok. I don't really see why that would bother you."

"It bothers me because when we found out, Keith acted like he knew what was going on. But he didn't really wanna tell me. What the fuck, man? Y'all leaving me out of the circle or something?"

"Dude," Mecca began, "since we were little you've been disappearing at weird moments and shit. We just chucked it off as you learning new skateboard tricks or something."

"I get that. I totally get that. But I just got a weird feeling about whatever is going on. Let me know what's going on."

107

"It's nothing, bro.

"Alright man," Sammy said exiting the room. "I'll get at you later."

As Sammy left, Mecca wondered why that was such a big deal. He grabbed his jacket, his bookbag, and quickly walked out of the door to head to class. The whole time his mind was just on what would happen next. When he finally got outside, he saw Shelby sitting with a deep brown-skinned guy on a bench.

"Shelby?" Mecca said walking over to her. "It's not Thursday yet, why are you here?"

"You're Mecca?" the guy asked. He had two eyebrow rings in the left brow along with eight earrings in his left ear.

"Yeah," he answered. "Who are you?"

"I'm Seven," the guy told Mecca.

"That's your real name?" he asked him.

"Yeah," he replied. "Seven Wilkes."

"We're here because we have to pull you out of school for a few," Shelby told him.

"A few what?" Mecca asked. "Hours?"

"Days," she told him.

"Are you serious? I've got class in like five minutes."

"Forget class. You're coming with us," Seven said. "Apparently Sabbath got wind of the fact that Tevin was kind enough to transfer his light to a long-haired natural kid attending VCU."

"Who the hell is Sabbath?" Mecca asked.

"That's the opps, Mecca!" Shelby yelled in frustration. "He leads the Earthers. Pay attention! Now stop arguing and come the hell on before we beat the shit outta you!"

Mecca was about to yell back in defense, but then he thought back to Rita's warning about what would happen if he gave Shelby a rough time. After he thought about that he looked up at Shelby and Seven, who were waiting on a response.

"We can fight if need be," Seven told him calmly. "I just don't give a fuck."

"Alright, I'll go with you guys," Mecca said. They started walking off. That's when Sammy started walking towards them, stopping mid-step. He gave a strange look to Mecca and his companions.

"Hey, Sammy," Mecca said. "I'll get up with you guys later, yo. I got, uh, some things I gotta handle."

Sammy didn't say anything. Mecca looked at Seven and Shelby. Their eyes were locked tight onto Sammy as if he were some kind of target of theirs. Mecca's heart began to pound profusely. Something wasn't right.

"Seven," was all Sammy said. Seven smiled at him, but it wasn't a kind smile in any way whatsoever. It was at that point that Mecca realized two things. The first was that Seven and Sammy most certainly knew each other. The second was that Sammy was a fucking Earther.

"You wanna try something here, Sammy boy?" Seven said with that vicious smile. "You know I don't give a fuck."

"C'mon guys, let's go," Shelby said grabbing Seven's arm. They all began to cross. As Sammy walked past, he looked at Mecca with a cold look. It was startling. Mecca had never seen him look like this before. He could feel their friendship deteriorating in that very moment. Then it was over. They kept walking.

They got only a few feet further when Seven turned around quickly and smacked a rock that was about to hit the back of Shelby's head. For a second, Mecca was worried that someone may have noticed the small piece of light that emitted from Seven's hand when he rejected the rock from the air. But no one was looking in their direction until he started walking angrily towards Sammy, who had his hands up to antagonize them.

"Throwing rocks though, Sammy!" Seven shouted while throwing off his jacket. "Let's go!" He pushed Sammy back and threw a right hook. Sammy dodged that and the next few punches. Shelby ran over to grab Seven's jacket, and then she pulled Seven away from Sammy before things got worse.

"I got you on the battlefield though," Seven said as Shelby pushed him away. Everyone who was walking past had stopped to see what all of the commotion was about.

"Fuck you, Seven," Sammy said walking backwards with his middle fingers up. "Yo, Mecca! I hope they teach you well! You're gonna need it!"

"C'mon, Seven!" Shelby shouted angrily at her comrade. "Dammit! I swear on everything, working with you is like babysitting a freaking three-year-old, man. Damn!"

They hurried from the main promenade of campus, where the commotion had been. The three Lighters walked in silence until they came to the old abandoned subway.

"I'm sorry, Knox," Seven finally said to Shelby. "But in my defense, he was gonna hit you in the head with a rock."

"Whatever," Shelby responded, waving her hand dismissively. She turned to Mecca. "How do you know him?"

"Sammy?" he asked quickly.

"Yes," she said sternly. "How do you know Sammy Hedges?"

"We grew up together," Mecca told her. "He's my best friend... so I guess this is why he used to disappear all of the time."

"That's exactly why," Seven said. "Most Universians develop their powers between ages six and ten. If he never told you, then he just never wanted you to know. Not your fault."

"I'm sure he picked up on the signs of your transformation though," Shelby stated. "He's more than likely the one that told Sabbath about it."

"Wait," Mecca started, "if Universians develop their powers, then how did..."

"Well, Lighters are the only ones who can transfer our powers into a natural Human," Shelby explained. "But only if we're on the verge of death."

"Yeah," Seven said chuckling. "Shelby should know. "

"Shut up, Seven," Shelby said with a mean look shot at him. She looked back at Mecca. "C'mon, Mecca. We've gotta get you up to par for what's in store kid."

"Okay," Mecca said with a sigh. "I'm ready."

Universe Glow: The Comic Book Series
Issue #1: The Universians

AVAILABLE NOW ON KINDLE

CHAPTER SEVEN

FALL OF A NEPHILIM

It didn't go as planned. Binsy thought for sure that he'd be able to get Laura and Ricardo to safety in Brazil, but unfortunately they'd been ambushed by the archangel Gabriel and two other Power ranked angels. He wasn't sure if Laura, the love of his life, had survived the attack or not. Ricardo was surely gone. Seeing his friend's floating, lifeless body was an image that would be burned in Binsy's mind forever. He'd been walking around destroyed mountain rubble for fifteen minutes, yelling for Laura. Regardless of this, Binsy knew that he wouldn't be able to find his lover if he wasn't able to think straight. He spread his wings, fighting through the pain extending them caused on his ribs and back, which were bruised to the max, and flew into the cloudy, rain-filled, thundering sky.

All he could feel in his soul was hatred and, in all honesty, confusion. Why did the angels seem to want his kind, the Nephilim, dead so badly? There was so much evil amongst both natural and supernatural creatures, but it seemed as if the angels only made their presence known when killing Nephilim, the forbidden offspring of Humans and fallen angels. As far as Binsy knew, there were as many reports of angels killing witches and Eartians as there were reports of Universian sightings. None. But at least mortals knew that Universians existed. Angels and demons? Nephilim? These were just fables in the minds of all Earth-born creatures. From what Binsy had learned, from what he's lived through, the Powers were the rank of angels from Heaven that were tasked with killing his kind regardless of their sins or character. For him to have survived for as long as he had was nothing short of a miracle. But it felt as if this may be his last go at living.

Hovering from above, Binsy looked around the mountainous area hoping to see something, hoping to feel her presence. There was nothing. All he saw was flashes of lightning. All he could hear was thunder rumbling around him. All he felt was rain slapping his scraped up skin, each droplet fueling his rage more and more. His ribs were already trying to heal themselves, he could feel his bone atoms at work. Even still, he knew that it would take a few days to fully recover, which was time that he didn't seem to have.

Binsy wanted nothing more than to continue his search for Laura, but he was drained. He knew he needed to rest. Upon realizing this, he suddenly began to sense the energy of a celestial being, that was far too immense to be his woman's. When he turned around, he saw what it was that he'd felt.

Standing on the head of a large, white griffon with purple symbols painted onto it in Enochian, the language of the angels, was the archangel Gabriel. He gave Binsy a cringeworthy smile that made the young Nephilim shiver. The archangel pulled out his three-foot purple horn and blew into it, a battle sound. With utmost confidence, Gabriel spread his own magnificent six wings of light. He floated from the griffon's head, moving closer to Binsy.

The giant creature flew away from the scene, bolting upwards through the clouds leaving behind a flash of blinding light. The rain bounced off of Gabriel's purple gem filled, silver chest plate armor. The steel-like fabric of the white warrior robes the archangel wore, soaked up the rain, Gabriel didn't seem to mind. He then ripped off the right sleeve of his shirt, revealing an Enochian tattoo. Gabriel's purple horn then turned into a large black scythe with a blade that seemed to be made of a purple amethyst, much like the ones in his armor. The scythe as a whole soon began to have a very vibrant and violent violet glow to it. Binsy smiled. Soon he was laughing out loud even though his ribs hurt. He knew he was about to die. But he wasn't about to go down easily.

There was enough pain in his body to scream for an eternity, especially with his ribs and back being so busted up. But Binsy used the rest of his energy to engulf his entire body in the pink, green, blue, red, and white flames of heavenfire. He was now a walking weapon. He charged at Gabriel as fast as he possibly could, prepping his right fist to do damage to the archangel's perfectly sculpted face. Gabriel swung his scythe before Binsy could even get in arm's length of him. The gust of wind from the scythe's blade stopped Binsy in his tracks and put out all of the heavenfire he placed around his body. The wind also slashed his left eye, cutting him to the bone and blinding him in that eye from the gush of blood that would come from it. Next, he felt the thick bone of angel knuckles bury themselves in the bridge of his nose. Blinded in one eye, the pain of a now broken nose, a sore back, and busted ribs, were all of the right ingredients to put young Binsy in a daze. As his vision became blurrier, the demi-angel's wings retracted. There was no way for him to focus on keeping his wings lit anymore.

As he fell out of the sky, Binsy felt Gabriel's scythe blade impale his chest. His body immediately went into shock. The fanatical archangel flew downwards, racing to the mountainous terrain below them and pressing the Nephilim's body into the ground at a violent speed. From a distance, the impact of Binsy's body hitting the mountain looked like a comet hit it, leaving a crater in the landscape. His foot now on Binsy's chest as he lay near lifeless on the Brazilian mountain, Gabriel broke the blade of the scythe off into the Nephilim's chest. The archangel faced the sky and smiled, seeming to relishing in the moment of his victory. His wings still spread, he flew high into the sky.

Binsy looked beside him, seeing that one of the rocks beside him was split open. Inside of the rocks were purple amethysts. Binsy chuckled a bit, now understanding why Gabriel's power seemed to be enhanced. He then turned his head upward, looking at the cloudy sky as raindrops hit him in the face. He was beginning to fade. As his right eye began to close for what he was sure would be the last time, he saw the silhouettes of two people standing over above him. Both of them had long hair, but one of them held an oddly shaped, swirled cane with an ankh at the tip. He didn't care about why they were there. They were too late. Gabriel had gotten to him first. Binsy closed his good eye, preparing to die. But he was jolted awake from feeling his insides become scorching hot. He felt an explosion begin in his stomach.

Melodies were sung above him, and then Binsy was engulfed in purple flames.

CHAPTER EIGHT

DIAGNOSING MR. FENTON

Dr. Deidre Dunham sat quietly at her desk dressed in her favorite black work dress. She was reviewing the symptoms that a potentially new client had informed her of experiencing. This particular person, a sixty-seven year old white man named Alexander Fenton, had called Deirdre about four days prior insisting to set up an appointment for the soonest available time slot. Due to something she felt in the man's voice when he spoke, Dr. Dunham arranged a time to see this man. The only symptom he'd given her was the three letter word, "sad".

Alexander Fenton stepped into Dr. Dunham's always welcomingly warm office at 3:15pm that Thursday afternoon. The quality of his attire, a blue denim jacket with a grey collared shirt with and black denim jeans to match his black chelsea boots, made Dr. Dunham take notice of the man's financial class. Though she could vividly see that his spirit was dimming, she felt as if she were dealing with a very powerful person. Before Mr. Fenton took his seat, he nodded at the respected shrink. Suddenly, she was able to recognize what she felt when she heard him speak over the phone. Peace. The same sense of peace Mr. Fenton was causing Deidre to feel was something she'd only felt from a limited number of people during her strange childhood. Only God knows how tough it was to get peace from her mother.

"Hello, Mr. Fenton," Dr. Dunham said. "It's nice to finally meet you."

"How's it going, Dr. Dunham?" Mr. Fenton replied in a smooth, low, gravelly voice. "It's nice to finally be here."

"So, would you like a second to get settled in or would you rather get started right away?"

"I'd definitely like to get started now," he assured her.

"Great," Dr. Dunham said with a soft but firm smile. "So, when did you start feeling this sadness?"

"It started a few months ago," he told her. "I started realizing that the world is a bit flawed, for lack of better words."

"So the world is making you sad?"

After pondering the possibility for a moment, Fenton responded by saying, "More or less. I would say I'm more so disappointed with the way that the world turned out. When I was younger, I never imagined that it would be this way."

Dr. Dunham cocked her head to the side curiously and said, "Well, what was your life like growing up?"

Alexander Fenton sighed. He closed his eyes tightly for a brief moment, searching for memories stored deep, deep down within the vaults of his mind. After quickly bringing them to the surface, he said, "I had an extraordinarily happy childhood. My mother was what you would call a gardener of sorts. She grew the most beautiful plants and fruits and vegetables that anyone in the world had ever seen. People came from all over just to taste her papayas."

"Were you close to your father?"

"Oh, very. He was strict, in a timely sense, I mean. Very punctual."

"What was he?" Dr. Deidre Dunham asked curiously. "What did he do for a living?"

"I always saw him as a theorist or a philosopher. In actuality, he was a chemist by trade. He used to joke about how he would crack the code of the universe one day."

Dr. Dunham chuckled a bit.

"How'd that turn out for him?" She asked him.

"He cracked it," Fenton said flatly, tone very serious. "It was completely on accident. But he definitely cracked it."

"Is that so?" Dr. Dunham said, suddenly even more interested in her new patient. She jotted down a few notes, he might be delusional.

"What did he find out?" She asked him.

"If I told you that, you'd die. Right here on the spot. You'd cease to exist because there would be nothing more to learn in this life for you."

Dr. Dunham found herself a bit thrown off by Fenton's response. "Oh, okay then. Well, your father sounds like a brilliant man. Might I have heard of him?"

Mr. Fenton shifted in his seat a bit, seeming a bit awkward about answering the question. "You've heard of him. Just not in a recognizable sense."

"Well, what was his name?" Dr. Dunham asked with false curiosity.

"Chrono," Fenton answered. "My father's first name was Chrono."

"Really?" Dr. Dunham asked in confusion. Then, almost unsure if she even should, she asked, "Was your mother's name Earth?"

"No," he said. "Her name was Terra."

Deidre paused for a moment, totally baffled by the delusion of the man sitting across from her. Dr. Dunham leaned forward and seriously asked, "Is this supposed to be some kind of joke, Mr. Fenton?"

While sitting in his chair in an almost father-like demeanor, he sighed and said, "Deidre, you've been waiting to hear something this interesting from a patient for the entirety of your career. This is it, right here. And no, it's not a joke at all. It's something that I've decided that you deserve to hear. So, are you willing to listen? And please make note that I already know what your answer's gonna be."

Deidre Dunham sat in her chair silently for a brief moment. She clutched her pen and notepad, but wrote nothing until her mind had completely halted its rattling thoughts.

What the hell had she gotten herself into? Was the Fenton fellow just speaking nonsense? Or was she in fact about to listen to the strangest backstory she'd ever heard in her life? Regardless, she was indeed there to listen and diagnose. It was her job, and the session had already been paid for. And though this patient seemed to be a perfect concoction of delusional and insane, there was a small part of her that believed this story was true.

"Please," Deidre said, composing herself, "carry on."

"I'm not really sure where I left off," Mr. Fenton told him.

"Your parents were named Terra and Chrono. The latter of the two supposedly cracked the code of the universe."

"Yep, that's right. And as ironic as it may sound, it's the truth."

"So what happened after your father cracked this universal code?"

"After the code was cracked, a new one began to form. A new universe, I mean. That's just the rules of creation. It was time for a new universe to form. As soon as someone figures out the code to the universe, which is the purpose of that universe's existence as a whole, that universe will begin to rapidly deteriorate. My father went to the head of every country on my planet, but they all thought that he was out of his mind."

Dr. Dunham shook her head at the information she'd just received. There was no possible way that this man, as calm and put together as he was, was any form of the word sane. If by some chance he were, it'd be because he truly believed the extravagant scenarios that had obviously been developing for so many years within his own mind.

"Forgive me," Deidre Dunham said. "I hate to challenge your story, but did you say, 'your planet'?"

"Yeah," Fenton replied.

"That would imply that you are in fact not from this world."

"Precisely."

Dr. Dunham sighed with relief. It was public information that the Eartians are a hybrid people born from the interbreeding of the American slaves and Martian refugees in the early 1800s, just as it was public knowledge that the Elves were descendants of the Pleiadian people that arrived to Earth during the reign of the Egyptian empire. So in her mind, this older gentleman being an immigrant from another planet, even if it's one that our Earth wasn't very familiar with, was an actual possibility.

"Okay," she said with a smile, "that makes more sense. I thought that this was going somewhere else for a second."

Mr. Fenton chuckled, "Would you like me to continue?"

"I would most certainly like for you to."

"Damn right you do baby," Mr. Fenton said proudly.

"Come again."

"So yeah," Fenton said hurriedly, "my father stood before numerous councils explaining his discovery. In short, our entire solar system was going to destroy itself. They didn't take very well to hearing that."

"What were the initial reactions?" The psychiatrist asked.

"Eh, I don't know. I was only about nine or ten years old at the time. You know, to this very day I still have no idea about the in depth details of that meeting. Weird that I don't, considering those meetings were very vital to my life. But what I can tell you is that my original home had only five and a half years left to live from the time my father made his initial find."

"That's enough time to enjoy life," Dr. Dunham replied. "At least your people didn't die right away. Were you scared?"

"You would think that I would have been," Fenton told her. "I guess I was too, for a while. But after about two years or so, I found myself accepting it. Being that I was a child, I was considered an apocalypse baby, growing up in the end of the world. I started to make it a point that I was doing it right."

"Doing what right?" She asked him.

With a strange glow seeming to come from his green eyes, Alexander Fenton said happily, "Live. I lived. I jumped from wings of flyer fleet ships. I went into our jungles and turned one of my region's largest wild cats into my personal pet. I traveled. I joined what this world would consider a local newspaper, but I did so in every city that I decided to stay in for longer than a month. Creating those articles gave way to so many adventures. I just lived."

"Sounds like a lot," Dr. Dunham said as she took off her eyeglasses, which were beginning to fog for some strange reason. She wiped her lenses with her dress before placing them back on her face. "Did others have your mindset, or no?"

"A few people, not many. I don't think that anyone else went to the extent that I did to make sure I got in all of my desired experiences. I mean, I really became a nomad. I didn't stay in one place for anything longer than an Earth year and a half. I had a small bag of clothes, the only consistent garments were pants. I danced, drank, and smoked with all kinds of people. I truly fell in love with the creation of the world. With people. With life. I was in love with it all. And since peace was something that my people were wired for, it made my love that much stronger. So when our sky started cracking, I was already in a pure place. Spiritually speaking, I mean. I was also in—"

"Sky started cracking?" Dr. Dunham asked abruptly.

"Yes."

"What was that like," she asked him, "seeing your sky split itself open?"

Mr. Fenton closed his eyes and smiled, seeming to remember his home world. He took a few deep breathes then he opened his eyes and smiled at her.

"Our atmosphere's chemical makeup gave us a bright white sky when our sun was up," Mr. Fenton said. "It was similar to yours, but that was a key difference. And the stars looked neon green during the day. And we had a considerably normal night sky, black with orange stars. But the cracks in the sky--"

"Forgive me for cutting you off again," Dr. Dunham said.

"It's fine. What is it?"

"Before you go any further there are some things I'd like to ask you. Could you tell me more about this world of yours? What was it called, The traits? Things like that."

"I'd rather not say the name," Mr. Fenton said, actually frowning for the first time since he'd stepped inside of her office. It's heartbreaking to even write it out. And other than the white sky it looked a lot like this world, but it flourished much more richly in numerous ways. Greener grass that always held a purplish tint at the tips. Clearer waters. Cleaner air. It looked very much like this one when it was in its early stages. We never polluted our planet."

"What were the people like?"

"A hell of a lot nicer," he said with a chuckle. "We weren't Human, or Eartian, or any of that stuff per say so our genetic primal instincts were different. We were a peaceful people to our core overall, much like the Elves of this world. My mother was probably the most peaceful of them all. She had this pair of round earrings that were little orb-looking jewels. One was blue, the other green. As you can see, she has been a strong source of aesthetic inspiration for me."

"If I may, I'd like to ask a question," Dr. Dunham chimed in. "Your mother obviously represents the earth, since you're apparently speaking metaphorically. I have to know, you chose earth to represent your mother and time to represent your father, why so obvious? And how does this relate to you being sad?"

Mr. Fenton chuckled and sighed.

Looking at the shrink in front of him he said, "They represent these things because these things, earth and time, are based on them. Not vice versa. I wanted the memory of my parents to be represented diligently, so I based both concepts on them."

Dr. Dunham looked at her patient with confusion. What was he saying exactly? Once again this man, this Alexander Fenton, suddenly seemed a lot more likely to be crazy. But he seemed too emotionally attached to the details of the story to be lying. Could this man be so delusional that he actually believes that he's...

"Hey," Mr. Fenton said. "You seem to be thinking mighty hard over there. Is there something that you're thinking about asking me?"

"Are you...?" Dr. Dunham asked curiously.

"Yeah," Fenton responded in an enabling tone. "Go on. Spit it out and ask."

"Are you implying that you're God?"

"Would you really believe me if I said that I was?" Fenton replied smiling with acknowledgment.

Dr. Dunham was puzzled. There was no possible way that this man could be who he was implying himself to be. If he was, her unusual abilities would make it so that she'd know immediately. This was turning out to be a much stranger case than ones she'd previously encountered, and she'd had plenty of intense cases find their way into his office, but Alexander Fenton took the cake. A man strongly convinced that he's God. This must be a joke of some sort, Deidre thought to herself.

'*There's no way this old ass man actually believes he's God,*' she thought to herself.

"I don't have to believe that I am God," Mr. Fenton said in a very acknowledging tone, "I just am."

'*Did he just read my mind?*'

"Something like that," he said to her. "It all depends on how you look at it. If I am God, then to me, would you think that your mind is really yours? Or, is it just an extension of myself imprinted and extended onto you? Because if that's the case, then you're one with everything because you're one with me. And that would technically make your mind, my mind as well."

"So you know what I am thinking?" Dr. Dunham asked him, placing her pen down on her pad for it to stay for the rest of the session.

"From your perception," Mr, Fenton responded, "yes, I know what you're thinking."

"Can you tell me where I grew up?"

"I could, but I mean c'mon," Mr. Fenton said with a laugh, "that's too easy. You would just assume that I looked up information on you. I just don't see the fun in taking obvious routes. Never have."

Dr. Dunham cocked her head to the side curiously. She started to reach for her pen to take some more notes, but when she felt another strange wave of peacefulness flow through her body, she put the pen back down. Looking up at Alexander Fenton, the man claiming to be God, she asked, "Exactly how long has it been since you stopped taking these 'obvious routes'?"

"Bold question," Mr. Fenton said with a slight chuckle. "You have to remember, I wasn't always 'God'. At one point, I was just a fifteen year old kid who'd lost everything they loved but in return was granted an infinite amount of power. So in the beginning, I was just sort of creating for the sake of creating. I was experimenting with my own thoughts; seeing where my imagination took me, stretching the boundaries of my power."

Dr. Dunham noticed her hand began shaking.

"What was it like? Having such a high burden at such a young age."

"Well, it was rough of course," Fenton said. "I was just starting my life. That was the age that kids became independent in my culture."

"That's still the culture that you claim?" Dunham asked curiously.

"It's the one that shaped me into the...entity, that I am today. Every religious idea that ever sprouted up in someone's mind, some piece of it came from my tradition. It was called Ono Timpâ, which in my language meant The Oneness."

"Wait, you said that religious ideas sprouted in people's minds? What do you mean by that?"

"I'm not as directly responsible for religion as people would like to believe," Fenton continued, "not fully anyways. How people choose to perceive me is ultimately on them. It all starts from the feeling that there's something out there greater than yourself. The God-Gene. All sentient lifeforms have it, though some are more active than others. I placed it there as kind of a branding symbol. Like 'Made In China' is to America."

"That's more so a form of recognition," Dr. Dunham stated. "Not branding."

"Isn't it?" Alexander said with a sneaky smile on his face. "The thing with my little signature, was that it gives you all the initial sense that there's something greater than what you could ever imagine out there. Then it just sort of develops into written wonders about what I'm like and what I want from you. To be honest with you though, Deidre, no one has ever come close to knowing how far off they are about knowing what it is that I want."

"Okay," Dr. Dunham said, gathering her thoughts. "So basically, we have it all wrong. Islam? Christianity? Judaism? Buddhism?"

"Buddhism actually happens to be the closest."

"Really?"

"Really."

"How so?"

"They understand that they don't understand. That's the most important step in understanding what I am."

"So in order to understand God, we must understand that we don't?"

"Yes," Fenton said. "You must also understand that you will never fully understand the person next to you either. But when you begin to fully understand yourself, not only as a person, but as a being, you then begin to grasp me."

"Okay," Dr. Dunham said, taking another deep breath. "Mr. Fenton, could you elaborate more on when your father cracked the code of the universe? I'm sure there had to have been some kind of mass panic to this discovery."

"There definitely was," Mr. Fenton began. "My world wasn't exactly ready for the news. Initially everyone thought that my father was crazy. But the more he explained himself, the clearer everything became. Everyone's minds began to open up for the first time. It was our highest point as a race. There was a short lived era of complete, total, and utter love that lasted about two Earth years or so of it. Not just peace. Love. Everyone genuinely cared for each individual person for the life form that they were. And all of a sudden, everything ended up falling back on me."

"What do you mean by that?" Dr. Dunham asked him.

"By what?"

"By everything falling back on you? What do you mean by that?"

"It means that when a universe comes to an end," Fenton began, "God *has* to choose a successor."

"I'm confused," Dr. Dunham said, this time with a slight chuckle. "I thought that you were God."

Alexander Fenton chuckled at her statement and sat back in his chair. His eyes began to dart around the room freely until he began to speak again.

"Yeah," he said, "but that doesn't mean that I always was. There was a source deity that created me. And just the same, a new source deity will emerge from this world. In time. The cycle must always continue."

"And why would God be sitting in my office talking about how sad he is?" Dr. Dunham asked him, almost sarcastically. "Am I this new source deity? Because I don't want that burden. If you really are God, you should be doing something to correct the enslavement of Black people and Martians that you let happen. Or maybe you should stop Wiccans from flexing their power whenever they leave their precious shadow society. Or what about the Universians? They're busting up the whole damn world right now and everyone is too damn afraid of them to even acknowledge their little civil war is destroying the planet. When there is so much you could be taking care of, God, why are you talking to me?"

"Because this universe's time is almost up," Mr. Fenton said with a smile. "Your world won't end because someone discovered my universal code, I made sure of that. But people have indeed decided to hack some this universe's energy through rituals to break the seals that I had in place to keep this particular universe together."

"Why would anyone want to destroy this universe?" Dr. Dunham asked in genuine confusion. Like anyone she knew, it would only make sense that someone would want to destroy the world. She couldn't grasp that people would be out for the whole universe though.

"Most likely to force my hand into giving them power," Mr. Fenton said flatly. "But before the last seal breaks, there is something you have to do."

"I don't understand," Dr. Dunham said, removing her eyeglasses. She massaged the bridge of her nose and sighed. She had put up with this charade for long enough. "I'm a medium. I've been able to see spirits since I was seven years old, okay? If God were to walk into my office, I would be able to know that. Your aura was so dim when you first walked in."

"Simple masking of the energy," Alexander told her. "I'll drop the act now, baby."

Without giving her the time for a rebuttal, Mr. Fenton's black eyes had now turned purple and had taken on a full-blown glow. The dim aura Dr. Dunham saw from the old man's soul when he first arrived, morphed into what the psychiatrist would count to be twenty large wings made of light. Before her very eyes, Mr. Fenton's skin began to darken. A third, glowing purple eye appeared in the middle of Mr. Fenton's forehead. His hair, which was short and white as snow, darkened to a jet black color. It grew into a long, flowing, kinky bed of hair as long as the locs touching Dr. Dunham's waist. Mr. Fenton's clothes had burned away in a burst of purple, sparkling energy.

With an extra two inches of height, and a large bust that now sat where a flat chest once was, Dr. Dunham was now staring at the most beautiful being she'd ever seen in her life. Flower bearing grass had grown at the bottom of God's feet, with strong brown roots wrapping around her shins. Butterflies fluttered about Dr. Dunham's office now.

Dr. Dunham was a medium. She'd traveled to other spiritual realms, she'd mastered astral projection, and she'd seen things that no one would ever believe. In a world filled with aliens, humanoids, fertile hybrid sentients; in a world where a human was able to see the spirits of the past, she'd never seen anything quite like this. Dr. Dunham stood up, prompting the beautiful being across from her to do the same. The psychiatrist dropped to her knees. Tears began to flow down her face.

"You're...you're..." was all she could manage to say.

"My child," God said, her voice sounding like the perfect women's choir, "Deidre Juniper Dunham. Born in Hampton, Virginia on June 18th 1974. The second of two children. The third medium of her family. You were shunned for your abilities by your own parents, but managed to overcome all adversities. You not only used your powers to become a wonderful, compassionate, psychiatrist. You've helped your country solve cases that would have been nearly impossible to solve without someone containing your gifts. You are the perfect liaison for what lies ahead."

With eyes full of tears, Dr. Dunham felt herself being lifted to her feet by her high creator. She looked her God square in her flashing purple eyes and smiled.

"What lies ahead?" She asked her. "How can I serve you?"

A smile on her beautiful, chocolate colored face, God said unto Dr. Dunham, "Be a mother."

www.ingramcontent.com/pod-product-compliance
Lightning Source LLC
Chambersburg PA
CBHW051346020726
47501CB00007B/2292